FLASHY GIFTS

AN OXFORD FLASH FICTION PRIZE ANTHOLOGY
IN PARTNERSHIP WITH THE UNIVERSITY OF
OXFORD'S BODLEIAN LIBRARIES EXHIBITION:
GIFTS AND BOOKS

F J MORRIS

CW00552023

First published by Oxford Flash Fiction Prize CIC in 2023.

ISBN-13: 9781739209735
AISN: B0CHWQC46J

CONTENTS

PREFACE

BY NICHOLAS PERKINS

Don't worry! You can get to the stories in a minute – the real gifts that this book contains. But before that, I want to say how delighted I am that the Oxford Flash Fiction Prize and the Bodleian Libraries have come together for this round of the Prize.

I'm the curator of the Bodleian's *Gifts and Books* exhibition, which has brought together books and other objects from a 4,000–year timespan, and across many countries and cultures. It explores not only books that were precious gifts, but also myths and stories about generosity, exchange and the power of storytelling to make a difference in people's lives.

This anthology has a similar scope and depth, and I've been both moved and excited by reading its brilliant stories. *Flashy Gifts* brings together writers from around the world, and they in turn give us the pleasure of entering the worlds that they create. They also remind us that every act of telling can also be a gift, provoking us to think and respond with a sharper glance or a larger heart.

I'm very grateful to all the people who've brought this book together: everyone who entered the Prize; the brilliant shortlisted writers; the fantastic readers and especially the judges Farhana Khalique and Patrick McGuinness; Neil Stevenson and Helen Cook in the Bodleian's public engagement team; and most centrally F.J. Morris, the Prize's inspiration and dynamo.

I really hope that you enjoy these stories and share them with your friends. Like many special gifts, they'll gain in value the more they're passed on.

JUST A LITTLE SOMETHING TO SAY...

Throughout the *Gifts and Books* exhibition at the Weston Library, University of Oxford, hundreds of people shared the stories behind a special book they had received, had given, or would give. They did this online, via comment cards, or on a gift tag in the exhibition space.

Each wonderful story showed how acts of gift-giving (and especially giving a book) are intimately bound up with wider social values, but also how they nurture our relationships with friends and family.

A selection of those real life stories we received are featured throughout the book, and we hope they inspire you.

PART I

POWER

'Watch me sing.'

I received *Homegoing* by Ghanaian African-American novelist, Yaaa Gyasi as a gift during my recovery from illness and I absolutely loved it. As a historian I loved the weaving of the characters around the issue of the transatlantic slave trade, including Jim Crow segregation up to present day. I have since bought copies for others as a gift but kept my own as a treasured copy.

My partner bought me Fredrick Backman's 'Anxious People' on a day I couldn't bring myself to leave the house. I have never been so moved by a book and it taught me lessons about empathy that have never left me since.

THE COSTA BLUES

BY EUGENIE BRYAN

Highly Commended for the New Voice Award

People ask why I choose the toilet of Leicester Square's Costa Coffee to practice my aria. I tell them it's because the acoustics in here are as good as any you can get in the London Opera House – and it's free. In any case, I can't practise my singing at home. I say home, but it's a shed where I sleep, head-to-toe, back-to-back, each night on a bed I share with my cousin, Samuel. He's from Eritrea too. We are not supposed to be here, so we creep around like ghosts, speaking in hushed tones, keeping our souls hidden, although our bodies are visible for those who wish to acknowledge us as human. Even when we slip out to our cleaning jobs in the City of London every day, we walk with bowed heads, trying not to leave alien footprints that give us away to those who don't want us here.

The shed is divided by a curtain down the middle, separating us from two other guys who take turns to share a large sofa that doubles up as a bed. They are from Syria and work shifts in local takeaway restaurants: Abdel, by day, Ahmed, by night. We get no natural light, as there are no windows in the shed, so we fumble around like skinny, blind mice most of the time, trying not to trip over the tangle of electric wires that snake through the ground, like a messy bowl of spaghetti. The only tunes I hear are from the birds tweeting in the trees outside at dawn; they sound like love messages being exchanged by lovers, like a call and response gospel. The kind of song I would love to sing to my girlfriend, Mariam, left back home.

Once, when I thought I was alone in the shed, and needed to rehearse the verse I had been suppressing in my chest, I raised my voice ever so slightly. Didn't realise one of the guys was trying to sleep under the heap of coats. He told me to 'shut the fuck up,' and to go and wail somewhere else, where people don't have to wake at 5.00am to earn their bread.

And now, the manager of the coffee shop is shouting:
'Are you alright in there, mate?'

What a stupid question, of course I'm alright. Never felt better, as I'm doing what I love. Okay, so I realise that it may sound weird to everyone else. Especially, as my last attempt must have sounded like the throttle of an old engine trying to get into the right gear, but I'm getting there. Just need to keep practising. I will never give up my dream to be an opera star. Like a scrawny Pavarotti, I can smell the applause of the audience, the encore, the garlands at my feet.

The handle of the toilet door is twisting up, now down, faster, more furious. Wait... nothing. Now, there's a hollow thud of fists bouncing off the door, in perfect harmony. Drummers rising to a crescendo, bringing the opera to a rousing chorus.

'Sir, I'm about to open the door. I've had complaints from customers who have been waiting to use the toilet for a long time now. It's now a matter of urgency that you leave. And you're making a lot of noise. Stand back!'

My friends, I am sending you this drama, live, via WhatsApp. I want you to know I used to practise my singing in Calais, as I made my way through The Jungle. You know, the refugee camp that they show on the news, where people live like rats, sheltering under damp cardboard boxes, knee deep in mud, as they try to escape to England on the back of a lorry. There are Afghans, Syrians, Nigerians, and Eritreans, like me. I tried 10 times to get onto anything with four wheels that would get me to England, but nine times I was caught. One night, I became a very good rat, burying myself into a lorry carrying cargo to England – I was 10th time lucky. Now I am here, nothing will stop me from achieving my dream.

I am not in your country for your food, or the weather. Just a little bit from your plate will do me just fine. Or so I thought when I first touched my feet on your soil. But now, having seen how some of you squander your good fortune, I want it all. Everything that you have, including the luxury of being obese and dissatisfied with my lot in a land of plenty.

When I was in The Jungle, the one thing I guarded more than my life was my mobile phone. Not because I wanted to contact anyone back home. Why would I want to tell them about my hunger, my fear of the others in the camp? My mobile now stays near my breast, like my abandoned love. I need to watch performances at La Scala, the Met in New York, and my favourite – the London Opera House. Places where all the big opera stars play. I need to listen to them for motivation. But I also want to study the gilded ceilings. Imagine the sweet scent of the wealthy sitting on soft, red velvet seats, sipping champagne during the interval. Passing judgement on singers, with bitter words of jealousy, on talent they will never possess.

Now, there are two people scraping me off the floor... like I'm a nobody. A bloody refugee. Ah, yes, you customers... all of you staring at me, mouths agape, as I am being pushed through the door... watch me sing. You are my audience, whether you like it or not, there is no escape. I will raise my voice until I start gagging. Higher, louder, until I feel my entrails rise to meet my ribs. They call me a public nuisance, but I am practising my craft. Even when they put me in the cell, I will sing and sing.

The Costa Blues by Eugenie Bryan © 2023

Eugenie currently works as a school librarian, but has also been a trade journalist and a lecturer in further education. After taking a couple of creative writing courses at CityLit, Eugenie discovered a love for creative writing. She was encouraged to continue honing her craft after receiving good feedback for her short stories. With retirement looming, Eugenie has been inspired to start a Substack newsletter: eugeniebryan.substack.com, exploring her next phase of life.

2

MOTHER OF EXILES

BY RAE COWIE

Highly Commended

Cheap imitations of the Statue of Liberty cluttered my childhood. The teak wall-unit, that stretched the length of the lounge, groaned under the weight of them. A polished bronze of the landmark sat proud on the windowsill, set on a pale marble base that glinted in sunlight. In the corner, where a lamp should have stood, a cardboard cut-out loomed, her torch flames licking the stucco ceiling. Sometimes, in the winter, I drew the curtains before it was dark.

When I was twelve, Mum dyed her hair copper and wound it into a Gibson Tuck. She stitched the statue onto cushions, and bought mugs and tea towels, fridge magnets and aprons. She removed the kitchen clock from the wall and framed a retro poster entitled, *Come to New York*. A stylised orange Liberty watched over me, as I crunched on jammy blackened toast. Our kitchen resembled a tacky gift shop.

'Most folks stop at one,' I said, embarrassed when friends muttered, 'weird'.

'One?' Mum snapped, spiky as Lady Liberty's crown. 'One is a *souvenir*.'

'Jeez,' Dad muttered, biting into a flaky bear-claw pastry. But still, each Thanksgiving, he wound fairy lights around the cardboard cut-out.

So, I did what I must to save face, and invented a Granny who'd set sail on a steamer from Boston and wore rubies and pearls on the voyage. Except, I had no Granny. No Grandad. No aunts. No uncles. No cousins. Mum had no family at all.

When I asked why, she said, 'People talk too much about families.'

I swiped three ornaments made of gaudy brittle plastic from the bathroom and ditched them in a bin at school. But by the weekend, five taller ones, longer than my forearm, had replaced them.

Summer and winter, day and night, a bulb shone bright as a beacon from our front porch, sending a beam beyond the pavement into the street. Inside, statues glimmered as Mum's knitting needles clacked, crafting scarves, beanie hats, ribbed fingerless gloves that were packed into shoeboxes then trucked over continents to warm refugees.

Each American Independence Day, she tugged a wide sheet from the airing cupboard and draped it around her torso like a stola. Then smiled, straight-backed, her face regal and smoothed. She seemed happiest robed, as Dad sprinkled weedkiller over patches of clover before mowing the lawn into definite stripes.

'I need a photograph of you as a baby,' I asked, 'for a project at Guides.' But she pretended not to hear. Not once did she show me a picture of herself as a child.

She spent one Christmas Day bent over the dining room table, constructing a replica of Liberty from sixteen hundred tiny plastic bricks, while Dad and I ate stodgy macaroni in the kitchen, watched by the turkey who sat blue with cold by the sink.

When friends discussed summer holidays, to beaches where fit guys sizzled on the sand, I never mentioned that Mum collected brochures, always saving for a trip to Liberty Island. Her dream, she said, was to kiss the Lady's green feet. The nearest Mum got was ripping out pages filled with photographs, which she pasted carefully into a scrapbook.

After college, I struggled to find the rent for the flat I shared.

'Can I move back... just until I get sorted?'

My voice was drowned by the rattle of the coffee grinder. Home-baked chocolate chip muffins, still warm from the oven, filled a plate; Lady Liberty napkins lay neatly folded on the side. It was Mum's afternoon when she welcomed local migrants, mothers with young children, who read well-thumbed copies of my favourite childhood stories. When *I* was little, it was Dad who read *Guess How Much I Love You,* as Mum diced carrots and added turmeric to lentil soup, which she served at charity luncheons.

She spooned the ground coffee into a pot and wiped her palms against her apron. 'Best stand on your own two feet,' she said.

'Mum?'

'Because that's what *I* had to do.' Her face crumpled, like George Washington's on a crushed dollar bill.

That evening, I flicked through grotty bedsits on my phone, as Mum sat, silent, on the opposite end of the couch, turning scraps of wool into a cosy blanket, as she watched a documentary about little children being smuggled from a Syrian camp. Weak and exhausted, their tiny frames appeared, crawling from the innards of an airless truck. Another and another, they kept coming. Some too limp to even sit, they collapsed across the gritty ground.

Mum bowed her head, tears soaking her croquet work, which trembled between her hands.

I reached for her fingers and squeezed.

'Did that happen to you, Mum?'

She shut her eyes and nodded.

The credits rolled, the programme almost ended, but it would never be over for Mum. I shuffled along the couch and placed an arm around her hunched shoulders.

At Christmas, I keep the lounge curtains wide, as the cardboard Lady Liberty twinkles in the corner. Mum wears the charm I bought, a tiny golden statue, threaded on a long chain so it sits next to her heart.

Each Saturday morning, I gather polish and fluffy dusters, and buff her collection until it sparkles.

Mother of Exiles by Rae Cowie © 2023

Rae Cowie is a short fiction writer with pieces published by the Bath Award, Cranked Anvil, Ellipsis Zine, Potluck Zine, Northwords Now, Postbox Magazine, Retreat West, The Great Scottish Canvas and more. She was thrilled to be granted a Scottish Book Trust Award 2022, and is busy editing her debut flash fiction collection. Discover more about Rae's work at www.raecowie.com

3

BUT AFTER THIS WEEK EVERYTHING WILL CALM DOWN

BY SAM RENNIE

New Voice Award Winner

—trying not to be one of those people constantly on their phone so I search *things to do other than be on your phone* and that's how I end up on my phone. *Do a puzzle*, it suggests. *Walk barefoot on wet grass. Start randomly screaming in public.* Then I get a notification about a storm that is apparently on the way; people are saying the vibes are *not good* and it has big *we're going to die* energy. Then I see a spoiler for a film that came out three hours ago, a sponsored ad for something that improves your memory, and a video of a dog with a crooked smile. When I look up, I notice I am in the queue for something. Then I'm sent a video about dissociating that will supposedly change my life and I reply *sounds amazing!!! I'll watch it later x* already forgetting what I'm talking about before I've hit send. Then there's someone saying another storm is approaching and someone else replying *that's the same storm you fucking idiot.* Then the queue shuffles forward. Outside, the weather looks normal: a slow-motion montage of the two remaining seasons. Now there's an account posting from the perspective of the storm and someone's put *I can't believe how disrespectful this is like people could die* and the account has replied *glup glup glup*. A live stream of the wreckage pops up and even though I'm watching it on mute, I can hear rainfall, sheets of consciousness melting away; like the time I used the torch on my phone to search my flat for the phone I was using; when I accidentally deleted a photo of my passport and panicked because I thought I had literally deleted the physical object; when I looked through old pictures and couldn't remember any of them, so I held the screen closer to my eyes as if I could sear the images into my brain and retroactively create the memories I clearly didn't form at the time. Then I realise the live stream I'm watching is actually the same five-second clip looping over and over so I close it and then I read a post from someone saying it's their birthday but they haven't spoken to anyone all day with thousands of comments underneath all wishing them happy birthday and then I read the storm account has been suspended for saying something racist so I quickly go back and unlike all of their posts and then I read that the storm is already here and when I get to the front of the queue and they ask for my name it takes me a minute.

But After This Week Everything Will Calm Down by Sam Rennie © 2023

Sam studied novel-writing at Bath Spa University and is from a small town in Essex where the roads are named after The Lord of the Rings — he grew up on Gandalf's Ride, a stone's throw from Hobbiton Hill and Rivendale Vale. In 2023 he was longlisted for the WestWord Prize. He is currently working on his debut novel and can be found on:
Twitter: samcsrennie | Instagram: samcsrennie

4

SOLVE THE PROBLEMS THAT FERGUS DENIES HE CAUSED

BY MALINA DOUGLAS

First Place Winner

1. When Mary leads the four-year-old child, wrapped in a shawl he singed the edges of when he started a fire in the kitchen, with a bracelet around one wrist printed in shaky letters the name *Fergus*, to the steps of the orphanage, kisses the small exposed brow and walks away without looking behind her, to what degree will the guilt eat up her insides?
Multiply the number of pinches by the number of tantrums and subtract from her love.

2. If each boy in the orphanage receives seven ounces of potatoes, and seven ounces of potatoes cannot fill Fergus' belly, how many boys must Fergus beat up to grow to his father's height of 179 centimetres?

3. When Fergus steps out through the workhouse doors at sixteen and three months, subtract from his feeling of elation fourteen rainy nights spent on Dublin streets, when he tracks down his mother to a crumbling tenement on Dublin's northside, and remaining in her cupboard are four teabags and

one and a half biscuits, and she justifies giving him up with seven anecdotes of his difficult behaviour, as she bites her lip and tears spill between her fingers, till she admits she has not heard from his father, or where to find him, calculate the depths to which Fergus' mood will sink.

4. Take the number of nights spent in fields, moors and the back of carts staring up at the sky and multiply by the number of stars visible on a clear night in Tipperary to find out the degree of yearning of Fergus for his father.

5. Take twelve rabbits, stolen, killed, boiled and eaten, twenty pickpocketed wallets and four dozen pilfered apples.
How many wrongs must Fergus commit to fill his inner abyss, formed by the feeling that nobody loves him?
5b. Calculate the square root to find the number of hearts he will break.

6. If Fergus has eyes like moss on an oak on the north side of a glade in Kilkenny, freckles on his cheeks equivalent to the number of sunny days he spent slacking off from farmwork (subtracted from an average of 168 rainy days in county Leitrim), has a laugh two semitones higher than the pitch of his father, is able to fire off three self-deprecating jokes a minute, and plays the fiddle at over 320 beats per second, how quickly will the average shopgirl fall for him?

7. If Fergus romances Brenda on the flowering cliffs of Howth, leads Molly into the grocer's storeroom, catches Louise behind a haystack and Evelyn in an orchard, multiply by three and divide by two outraged fathers, armed with pitchforks, who succeed in chasing Fergus away, how many cousins will Fergus' grandson discover in Galway?

8. If each child sired by Fergus grows up not knowing their father, three quarters of them are boys, and each boy starts a family of his own that he later abandons, how many pub fights can be traced back to Fergus?

9. If, on a rainy night in County Roscommon, Fergus walks into a pub and hears a man, twice his age, boasting that he knew how to deal with troublemakers since he sent his own son to an orphanage, and Fergus, upon asking the age of the son and adding the moss of his eyes and the freckles on his creased, ruddy cheeks, understands he is facing his father, and his anger can be calculated as the cumulative effect of thirteen years confined behind stone walls plus five years and seven months of ranging down muddy tracks, sleeping in fields and living off goods bartered and stolen, compounded by the rage inherited from his father who grew up without knowing his own father, and multiplied by four pints of Guinness and two shots of Locke's Special Edition, what is the likelihood that Fergus will punch his father in the face?

Write your answers on the answer sheet provided.
Answers left blank will be penalised.

Solve the Problems that Fergus Denies He Caused by Malina Douglas © 2023

Malina Douglas is inspired by the encounters that shape us. She was awarded Editor's Choice in the Hammond House International Literary Prize and longlisted for the Reflex Press Prize and the Bath Short Story Prize in 2022. In 2023 she was longlisted for the Bristol Prize and made the top three of the Leicester Writes Prize. Publications include the National Flash Fiction Day Anthology, WestWord Journal from Retreat West, Typehouse, Cast of Wonders, Wyldblood, Ellipsis Zine, Teach Write, Consequence Forum, and Because That's Where Your Heart Is from Sans Press. Her shortlisted writing was published by Blackwater Press and Desire to Escape from Four Palaces Press. She is an alumna of Smokelong Summer and can be found on twitter @iridescentwords.

5

LAST MAN STANDING

BY TONY WHITE

Content Warning: Violence

Teagan's feet scraped across the asphalt as he shuffled along the faded yellow line in the center of a quiet street. His rifle jostled against his shoulder as he walked, heavy steel knocking against bone and not much else. Duct tape wrapped around the toe of one of his standard-issue army boots swept up loose gravel as he kicked an empty soup can. With each bounce of the can, a ping echoed off the crumbling, bomb-struck buildings around him until it faded back into a silence that permeated the long-abandoned city. A silence deeper than ocean waters.

'It'd sure be nice to find a friend again,' Teagan said to the silent city. 'Someone to tell my story to.'

But there was no one. Teagan felt as if the whole world was holding its breath, afraid to answer and disturb the delicate peace. He shuffled up to the can again, letting the sling of his rifle slide wearily down his arm as he gave it another kick. The can echoed with a lonely hollowness that weighed heavily on

Teagan's shoulders, shook him at the knees, and brought him down slowly to the asphalt.

'After all the fighting and war there's nobody left to hear the story of it all,' Teagan said in a voice raspy with dirt and tears. 'And the last man standing is left to suffer alone. What was the point of it all? How did this happen? What does it matter now that none's left to care?'

Red rays of a setting sun glowed through the ruins of a firebombed building to the west. From the east, asphalt crunched gingerly under cautious boots. A shadow sprawled across the ground in front of Teagan, stretching down the yellow line in the street.

Teagan jumped to his feet and shouldered his rifle as he spun around in one fluid motion. So well trained that it took no thought at all. A man about Teagan's age stood centered between the notches of his iron sights. Tattered fatigues hung from his emaciated frame, not unlike Teagan's. His hands raised in a gesture of peace Teagan had become familiar with, but no longer trusted.

'Easy, my brother,' the man said. 'I'll listen to your story.'

'Stay back,' Teagan warned. 'Where did you come from?'

'I've been following you a hot minute, my man.'

Teagan's cheeks blushed. To be caught off guard and moping at the same time was not a good look for a soldier. Even a reluctant one.

'Why were you doing that?' Teagan asked.

'It's been a long time since I've seen another person. I waited until I was sure you were in the same spot as me. Put the gun down, brother.' The man stepped forward.

'Take another step and I'll shoot,' Teagan shouted. The rasp in his voice sounded like a guttural bark.

'You mean to tell me after all the fighting, you still got bullets in that rifle of yours?'

Even in the coolness of coming dusk, Teagan's forehead dripped sweat. 'Come closer and find out.'

'Alright, alright. Hot damn. You the same guy I just heard calling out for a friend?'

'How do I know you're a friend?'

The man stuck his hand out, calm and unshaken. 'We've got the same skin color do we not?'

Teagan looked at his own hands as they shook beneath his rifle.

'And I'm no woman either, am I?' the stranger asked.

'I suppose not,' Teagan agreed. 'What religion are you?'

'I don't believe in no god, my man.' He opened his arms and motioned to the crumbling world around them. 'Nobody does anymore.'

Teagan's eyes ran up and down the man's service uniform with jittery quickness. 'You're still suited up, though. Where's your party colors?'

'I gave them up. I'm through fighting, man. My fatigue is all I got.'

'What was your political affiliation?'

The man's eyes passed over Teagan, calm and patient, and came to rest on a colored armband over Teagan's right bicep.

'What does it matter, brother?' the man asked. 'Who cares what side I was on now?'

But Teagan knew better. He saw the look in the man's eyes when they stopped on his armband. He ground his teeth at the thought of the man's faux appeal to friendship. He squeezed the rifle tighter to his shoulder.

The man's jaw clenched. 'There's no need for that now.'

'This is all your fault,' Teagan whispered through quivering lips. 'It was your side that started it.'

'This is all our faults brother—'

The rifle popped and a bullet carved through the man's eye.

He hit the ground quicker than the smoking brass from Teagan's rifle.

Teagan let the gun drop and wiped the sweat from his eyes as he knelt to search the man's body. He found no weapons, but that made no difference. If his squad had been there, they would've congratulated him on a clean kill. It was him or the other guy, they'd say.

He continued searching and found no colors, no armband, nothing to indicate an affiliation to any political party. He may never truly know what side the man was on, but deep down, Teagan was sure he did.

He finished his search and found no photos, ID, or letters. The man was just another nameless body on a mountain made of corpses. More silence to add to the peace. Another breath held in for the rest of eternity.

Teagan stepped farther down the road to get away from the smell of blood and gunpowder. He slung the rifle back over his shoulder and looked down at his feet. Between his duct-taped boots, the empty soup can rolled in a gentle wind. He kicked it down the road and listened to the ping echo between the buildings. Then he walked after it.

'It'd sure be nice to find a friend again,' Teagan said to the silent city. 'Someone to tell my story to.'

But there was no one.

Last Man Standing by Tony White © 2023

Tony lives in Nashville, Tennessee in the United States where he works as a Security Guard in a High Security Juvenile Detention Center. Fun fact: this is actually his first writing competition! Originally from a small town in Wyoming, he mostly worked in construction until his early twenties when he put himself through audio trade school in hopes of working in music recording studios. He graduated and worked in several studios across many states until he eventually opened his own recording studio in Denver, Colorado, about 9 years later. Two years after that, he lost his hearing and sold his stake in the studio.

When he was 15, he did some time in a juvenile detention center, as did both of his little brothers. He decided that in this new chapter, he would do something to help troubled boys in need of guidance and this motivated him to start a new career of helping at-risk youth. He turned to writing, took a handful of online courses, and attended a couple of local workshops but hasn't had anything published until now.

PART II
—————
GENEROSITY

'It's one big block, the universe,
and everything is already there,
future, past, present.'

I'd give Joan Armatrading, *The Weakness in Me* as a gift. We went to see Joan in concert. As the support act was ill that night, Joan came on and covered. She played for about two and a half hours!

That night I was drawn into the lyrics of Joan's songs – a big range from fun and upbeat songs, to the thoughtful and moving. I love each page of the book!

I would give 'Braiding Sweetgrass' by Robin Wall Kimerer. Because it is so wonderfully written, I learnt so much from it and I would like to share this with others.

6

LUCK OF THE IRISH

BY LYNN EMBICK

It didn't end the way it did in fairy tales. Pauline was Irish, though, so she was used to that. People often mention the luck of the Irish, but don't always consider that luck is a two-sided coin, and the universe is forever striving toward equilibrium. With the good, comes the bad. Or, if you're really optimistic, with the bad, you can generally find a bit of good.

Pauline was born in 1925, in the hottest month of the driest year Oklahoma had seen in some time. She had two older brothers, seven younger, and one sister. There might have been an even dozen siblings, but they'd buried a baby in '34. When tornado sirens sounded, Mama had handed Pauline the newborn, and they all headed to the basement. Her mother and sister had huddled together on the other side of the dugout as the storm pressed down on them. Pauline had screwed her eyes shut, covering the baby's head, as the basement doors were torn away. When the wind died down, the baby wasn't moving. Doc said it was a rusty nail that had punctured a lung. Lucky Pauline wasn't hurt, he'd said. Mama never forgave her for that.

Life for tenant farmers wasn't easy. Eleven kids made their family appealing to some landowners, despite the brand of being Irish, and Papa always found them a place. Making friends was a challenge when you moved often and missed school to help make ends meet. Recently, Mama had informed Pauline that she would not be attending ninth grade. She'd done enough learning and her help was needed at home, with the little ones. Pauline tried to feel flattered, but it ached when the others headed to the schoolhouse, their reprieve.

Over the years, Sundays had become sacred, and now they meant even more. Pauline was in charge of ensuring her younger siblings attended church. Her older brothers stayed back to help Papa, and Mama generally slept in, saying she was in her vapours. It was at church, during Sunday School lessons, where she'd had the chance to get to know Lottie Parker, the daughter of the landowner who employed her father. Lottie was sweet, and for a few minutes each week, Pauline could pretend that they were two ordinary, giggly teenage girls, and that it didn't matter if the only two dresses she owned were made from flour sacks.

One fall Sunday, Lottie presented Pauline with a hand-me-down dress coat. Lottie brushed Pauline's protests aside, saying she got a new one each fall, and didn't Pauline look handsome in blue! Pauline ran her hands over the smooth material, and regarded the shiny metal buttons, as exquisite to her as if they'd been made of pearl. She accepted the coat reluctantly, not for lack of appreciation, but because of what she knew was coming.

When Mama saw the coat, she flew mad. She wanted to know what Pauline had said to make that Parker girl feel sorry for her. Then, she demanded that Pauline give the coat to her younger sister, Jewel. If any of them stood a chance of getting out of there, it was Jewel, and didn't blue bring out her eyes? Besides, she reasoned, Pauline would only ruin the coat with chores.

The next Sunday, Lottie was disappointed to see that Pauline was still wearing Papa's old barn coat. She inquired gently, worried that perhaps she'd offended Pauline with her gift.

Pauline tried to assure her that no offense had been taken. As church let out, and they exited the building, there was Jewel, surrounded by a few of the local boys, shining and laughing in her long blue coat.

Lottie took off her brand new coat, this one a deep red velvet, and handed it to Pauline. Pauline smiled sadly, avoiding the jacket and the conversation. She figured this would be the last time Lottie went out of her way to be kind to her. Gathering up her younger siblings, she began the long walk home. Jewel honked the horn of a suitor's bicycle as they passed, waving from her seat on the handlebars.

Pauline was halfway back to their tenant cabin when Lottie and her father caught up, and pulled their car over. Pauline had her youngest brother on one hip and the next oldest, a toddler, on the other. The rest trailed behind her like a train of stair-stepped ducklings, holding hands so as not to lose each other in the waves of wheat and corn. Mr. Parker offered Pauline a ride. She politely declined. Only after a stern rebuke at the state of her little parade did she allow the boys to pile into the back seat of the car, careful to keep their dusty shoes off of the upholstery.

When they drove up to the little shack, Mama was sitting on the front porch in her rocker, looking slightly more presentable than she did most days. Pauline profusely thanked Mr. Parker and tried to hurry her brood out of the car before a conversation could ensue, but Mr. Parker and Lottie headed straight for the porch. Papa and the boys came up just in time to hear Mr. Parker insist that Pauline be granted the gift of a red velvet coat Lottie was holding out. Mama frowned, but nodded her head at Pauline, who stepped forward to receive the coat. Mr. Parker, satisfied, escorted Lottie back to the car, and Pauline did her best to return Lottie's smile.

She listened as the sound of the engine faded in the distance. Mama emptied out her pipe, crossed the porch to take the coat from Pauline, and threw it into the burn barrel in the middle of the yard. As the flames engulfed the fabric, Papa joined Pauline, and put his arm around her shoulders. Silent tears ran down her smoke tinged cheeks, but a small smile played upon her lips. She had something Mama couldn't touch. Better than the coat, she now had a friend.

Luck of the Irish by Lynn Embick © 2023

Lynn Embick is a former children's librarian and classroom teacher, current freelance writer, and the author of the Substack, Mundane Magic. She has written multiple published poems, newspaper and magazine articles, and is an intermittent social media content creator and blogger. You can follow her work on Instagram, Facebook or Substack.

7

IF YOU LOOK AT IT ASLANT, MAYBE IT WON'T BLIND YOU

BY JO GATFORD

Highly Commended

The guy who thinks the moon landings were faked makes ramen like a Studio Ghibli movie and has beautiful forearms but some things are really difficult to get past.

'So, how?' I ask, on our second date, and he doesn't even need context—just sighs and starts making shapes with his hands, the way he does when he explains something he's passionate about, and it's like purple neon lines are stretching from his fingers, crafting invisible geometry out of the air.

'Look for the shadows,' he says. 'The angles. The flag. I mean, are you kidding me? This was nineteen-sixty-seven, they didn't even have green screen.'

For our third date, he invites me to watch the meteor shower. He brings wine and blankets and homemade samosas and when I ask him if he's a flat earther he laughs and says, 'I believe the moon is *round*, I just don't believe we've been there. Why do you think Neil Armstrong is always so grouchy? He's had to live a lie his whole life.'

It's cloudy and hard to see what's ancient rocks burning up in the atmosphere and what's just a passing satellite, but he pays the same precise attention to my body as he does his anime noodles and when he texts me later to see if I wanna hook up again I tell him, 'That's an affirmative, Houston.'

It's my turn, so I take him through the woods and up onto the hills for our fourth date. Of course he has proper hiking boots and a flask of coffee and can name the weird rolling clouds that look like paint strokes. 'What about chemtrails?' I ask. His answer is a kiss with smiling lips and even though our teeth clash, it doesn't matter.

The sky greys and we walk, hand in silent hand, until we find a dew pond between two hilltops. He cuts the glass surface with the toe of his boot and tells me a tale of folk trying to fish out the reflection of a full moon, thinking it was a wheel of cheese. 'That's why *moonraker* means idiot,' he says. I don't know if he's making fun of himself or me, but I take a gamble and order him a fancy cheese platter a couple of days later and he texts me twelve 'hysterical laughing' emojis in a row.

For a while there are no dates, just messages and phone calls and work and schedules that don't fit together, and when I'm not touching him—when I can't look directly into his Saturn-ringed irises—it gets harder to make excuses when my sister reminds me he's a conspiracy theorist. But the noodles. The hands. The night sky, mocking me every time it's clear.

'It's not like he doesn't believe in evolution,' I tell her. 'And it's okay to have differences in opinion with people you care about. You and I hardly agree on anything.'

My sister rolls her eyes back into white crescents. 'What are you gonna tell your kids when they go through their astronaut phase?'

'We've had four dates. There are no hypothetical kids.' I force a laugh but all I can think of is the kind of packed lunches he'd make; the serious softness of his reading voice; the way he'd look, sleep-deprived and bed-ruffled.

He calls me two seconds before I hit send on a message I've spent seven minutes composing—we read the same news story, shared the same idea, thought of one another before anything else—and he invites me over for espresso martinis on the roof of his building the next day.

'Bring a shoebox,' he says.

I empty out the stupid suede heels I've only worn once, to my sister's stupid wedding. And because he's not the only one who can be endearingly domestic, I make a batch of lopsided cupcakes, sprinkled with tiny sugar stars.

We sit in rainbow-striped folding chairs, my feet on his lap, and watch the shadows crawl across the grit. The air temperature slips a degree as darkness slowly eats the sun from west to east. 'Like Pacman,' I say, and then can't stop laughing because I'm three martinis down and his thumb is slowly massaging the notch below my ankle and maybe a few hundred years ago we'd be shrieking that the world was coming to an end but right now the eclipse feels like a giant wax seal of approval.

For a few minutes, the moon fits perfectly inside a circle of flame. We turn our backs on it and take turns peering into the shoebox. 'You have to aim it through the pinhole,' he reminds me, but I am an expert at not looking things in the eye.

The cardboard version is a little underwhelming—just a fingernail of light, daring me to turn and stare directly into the real thing until the truth reflects onto my retinas.

'Don't,' he says, because after five whole dates he can apparently read my mind, and he holds me still, hands cupped around my shoulders, and the moonshadow is so tiny and frail what does it even matter how many billions of dollars NASA spent to get there; how many Apollo missions blew up and which ones made it; if there are moon rock paperweights on someone's desk somewhere or if it was all shadow puppets in Kubrick's basement; if we'll live to see life on Mars before the earth scorches itself dry and how many light years all of it is away from this little roof and my underbaked cupcakes, so I turn—his body shielding me from whatever celestial ridiculousness is behind us—and even though I may never be able to believe the way he does, I realise I'm still prepared to flip the bird at the moon for the rest of my life.

If You Look At It Aslant, Maybe It Won't Blind You by Jo Gatford © 2023

Jo Gatford writes short things about strange things. Her work has most recently been published by The Fiction Desk, Cease Cows, New Flash Fiction Review and PRISM. She occasionally tweets about weird 17th century mermaid tiles at @jmgatford.

8

CHIAROS-CURE-ALL

BY OWEN TOWNEND

I may never have learned that my art could cure if my friend Jay hadn't asked me to sketch him. He was in the ICU, resting after another frustrating visit from doctors who had no idea what was ailing him. It had been like this for nearly a year and Jay was becoming visibly frailer each time I visited. My words of encouragement became a frustrating routine that meant nothing. What else could I do but agree to sketch him?

Right up to the moment I raised my pencil, I worried about what I would capture of Jay's current state and how it would make him feel. No-one wants to see themselves looking weak, especially when you don't know the reason why.

Still, after the initial clumsy strokes, you couldn't stop me. Something about the way the light streamed through the window and hit his jawline inspired me. Despite it all, Jay still had a strong chin, strong enough to help me get over the trepidation and just give my friend the present he wanted.

However, when I was done, the revisionist in me took hold. There were so many dark lines, shadows that needn't be there. I was back to worrying about how Jay would react and did my best to smooth out his grey sunken eyes and exhausted features.

As I showed him the sketch, one of the nurses approached to

refresh Jay's medication. I only had a minute to gauge his response.

'Lovely, mate,' he told me, tears peeking out the corner of his eyes. 'Cheers.'

Visiting time was over, but I left the sketch with him. I don't know where the nurse put it after I left but it can't have been far from his bed.

Overdue commissions kept me away until a couple of days later. When I walked into Jay's room, he was sitting up. He hadn't been able to do that since January. Not only this, he looked brighter. His eyes were no longer bloodshot, and his cheeks weren't hollow. The doctors had noted an optimistic change.

'No promises, though,' Jay joked. He said this with the excitable energy of a schoolboy awaiting a treat.

And yet his good health persists. Jay still has regular checkups, but his phantom pains have long since faded. As for the sketch I did, he hung it in his living room. I see it often but I still can't fathom it. Call it vanity, but it seemed there was something about my creative act that had changed things.

It put me in mind of Dorian Gray. Like the book, maybe I drew the decay out of Jay and, when I erased it, his strange sickness was gone for good. A ridiculous assumption, but one that kept sitting in the back of my mind. The prospect of preserving lives this way, improving them even, worked away at my better judgement for months. When I was finally on top of my commissions and approaching restlessness, I had time enough to try something that should be impossible.

I returned to the ICU during one of Jay's visits, sketchbook in hand. It took ten minutes for the nurses to go on a coffee break and even then I had to lure one lad out with a lie about an old fella coughing his guts up outside. Fortunately, this nurse was gone long enough for me to sketch a couple of the sleeping patients on the ward. Not my best work, but good enough for me to capture their likenesses. I might have gone overboard with the wrinkles, but then I had a theory about the thicker dark lines. Dorian Gray again. As with Jay, I rubbed these out with great care.

When I heard the shoes of the nurses squeak up the hallway, I tore out my sketches and laid each under the beds of the patients that inspired them. The nurses found me and told me to leave right away. I gave them some daft story about losing my watch while visiting Jay and thankfully they believed it long enough not to call security.

Meeting up again with Jay later, I told him what I had done.

'That's insane,' he replied with a hard stare. 'I wouldn't want any nosy stranger seeing me at my worst, let alone sketching it. You should have known better.'

Nevertheless, I begged him to make up an excuse so we could revisit the ICU a day later. Well, Jay would visit and I would stay in the car.

He shook his head but I could tell he was intrigued. Why else would he put my sketch in pride of place for everyone to see? He knew it had some sort of magic to it.

So the next day, Jay visited the ICU ward, bringing muffins to thank the nurses who had taken such excellent care of him. While they ate, he pretended to visit the loo, then looked in on the patients.

'They were all bright. Energetic,' Jay told me later in the car, with a bemused smirk. 'One even winked at me.'

So I was vindicated. Somehow, by setting pencils on paper followed by an eraser to clear away the darker lines, I could help people overcome grave health. The way I figure it, the dark lines must not be mistakes. They are the illness, shadows cast by death. Simply by erasing these lines from the sketch, I erase the ailment from the patient.

I know it sounds mad. Chiaroscuro is not a scan and erasing shadow from art can't be treatment. But there's something in it. Give me a chance and I'll show you. I can prove this isn't coincidence, magic or a miracle, but a new kind of science.

Take me to your sickest patient and I will draw them. I will draw the pain right out of them.

Chiaros-Cure-All by Owen Townend © 2023

Owen Townend is a writer of primarily short speculative fiction, but he turns his hand to poetry, script and nonfiction as well. He has been published by Comma Press, Twisted Fate Publishing and May Tree Press, among others. He is currently working on a series of Western novellas and is an active member of the Huddersfield Authors' Circle, the Yorkshire Writers Lunch and other groups.

You can read more about him at:
huddersfieldauthorscircle.co.uk/portfolio/owen
You can also follow him on Instagram: @omt144.

9

MY FATHER, RETIRED PHYSICS PROFESSOR, EXPLAINS IT ALL

BY EMILY RINKEMA

He says, 'It's one big block, the universe, and everything is already there, future, past, present.'

We are sitting at the kitchen island in his house, playing a new version of gin rummy that involves matching colors and dropping cards to the floor to see how they fall. He is winning. Or maybe I am winning, hard to tell. One of my roles in our new version is to pick the cards off the floor. I make a new pile in front of each of us. 'Your turn,' I say.

'Right now we are here in this kitchen,' he looks around. 'But we're also in my kitchen.' This is a new development, thinking that his house is not his house, that we are sitting in a kitchen that looks like his kitchen, but is not, that I am an imposter that looks like his daughter, but is not.

He continues. 'I'm both here and then,' he says, mixing place and time. He picks up his cards and looks at them. Rearranges them. Rearranges them again.

He has been explaining physics to me since I was a little girl, usually over cards, but sometimes over dinner, or in the car, or later, with drinks in front of the fire. He has tried to explain gravity, black holes, string theory, block theory. It's never been successful, but he hasn't given up, even when I failed physics in high school, even when I became an English major, even when I became a poet and married a painter. Once, when he tried to explain the concept of the expanding universe on the way to a soccer practice, I burst into tears. When he asked me why I was crying, I just shook my head because I was too scared to tell him that I couldn't sleep some nights thinking about a world with no edges.

I put down two red cards and then push them over the edge of the table. They fall together, but split when they hit the tile floor. He nods, scratches his nose.

'There is no time,' he says, and then, 'When is my daughter going to get here? She should be home by now.'

'I'm right here, Dad,' I say, and he looks up from his cards and into my eyes. He leans forward and squints.

'Nice try,' he says. 'Where is she?'

I know I'm not supposed to argue. 'She'll be here soon,' I say. 'Must be lost.'

He looks at his cards, selects one from the middle of his hand, and sets it in front of us. It's a four of diamonds. He slowly slides it to the edge of the table.

'All just points in the block, all there always, no beginning or end.' He tips the card over and it falls slowly, flips on the way down, lands under his chair.

'Makes no sense,' I say, and I am seven again, fifteen, twenty-two, thirty-six, hoping he will keep talking to me, but blocking out what he says so I can breathe.

'You're not trying hard enough,' he says, and then, 'My daughter gets it.' He places three more cards in front of him, two red and one black. He pushes the black one off the table and it falls straight down, lands face up beneath us.

'Gin,' he says, and then moves his hand from left to right in front of us. 'None of it is laminate.' Shakes his head.

He is getting tired, frustrated. 'Nothing ever ends.' And then, 'When can I go home?'

My Father, Retired Physics Professor, Explains It All by Emily Rinkema © 2023

Emily Rinkema is an educator and writer living in Vermont, USA. Her writing has appeared in The Sun Magazine, SmokeLong Quarterly, Phoebe, Sixfold, and in the Best American Nonrequired Reading Anthology. When not writing or working, she is most likely hanging out with her husband and dogs, reading, or watching BBC mysteries.

Twitter (X) and IG: @emilyrinkema

PART III

REVERENCE

'You just take your time.'

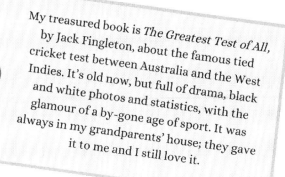

My treasured book is *The Greatest Test of All*, by Jack Fingleton, about the famous tied cricket test between Australia and the West Indies. It's old now, but full of drama, black and white photos and statistics, with the glamour of a by-gone age of sport. It was always in my grandparents' house; they gave it to me and I still love it.

I consider every book I've ever had from a Public Library as being a gift from society to me. Through our taxes & endowments everyone in our country can have the gift of a book, before returning it in the form of a gift to the next reader. Long live libraries!

10

HUMBUG SHARK

BY KATHY HOYLE

Highly Commended

On the funeral director's desk there's a jar of black and white humbugs. An old-fashioned glass jar with a shiny silver lid, like the ones you see in sweet shops of yore. And don't ask me why I use the word yore when I would never, ever use that word usually, it just seeped into the room of its own accord, alongside a thin woman in laced boots and a white cap and apron, stark against her high-necked black dress.

The woman has veined hands, which she uses to take those glass jars down from heavy oak shelves. She unscrews the silver lids and fills a bronze scoop with humbugs from the jars. She pours the humbugs onto an iron weighing scale. They clink-clink and the dish tilts. The woman tips the humbugs into striped paper bags, carefully folds the top of the bags and hands them to children in bright bonnets, while indulgent mothers look on. The woman has a kindly smile and a gleam in her eye. A gleam that says, you chose well, your decision will bring you happiness, well done you.

I wonder if her name is an old-fashioned one, a name of yore (what even is yore?) And I'm thinking maybe it's Marjory or Ethel or Mrs Ada Quinn. I wonder if Mrs Ada Quinn was taken to her final resting place from right here, in this very funeral home - established in 1913 by Messrs Banbridge, Bolton and Sons - and I wonder if the money from her family paid for those swirling gold letters etched onto the shop front window and I wonder if the humbugs on the desk were her humbugs, and are still.

I wonder why humbugs. Because humbugs are sharp, not soothing at all, they're sombre sweets that nip at the tongue. They taste like shit. I wonder if the slick funeral director is even aware that they're there.

The funeral director is talking, flashing small shark teeth, talking, endlessly, talking about colours, Dove White, Genteel Cream, Break of Dawn Blue, and now he's telling me about fabrics, silk, velvet, satin or calico and he leads seamlessly into caskets, oak, wicker, steel and cherry, and he's talking, still fucking talking, about flowers, lilies, orchids, roses or irises.

I wonder if Ada would sigh, like he does, if I took my time choosing things from her shelves. Or would she kindly make suggestions? Maybe not humbugs at all. Maybe she would carefully bring down each jar for me to peer into and inhale the sugared smells? Give me all the time in the world to consider the overwhelming myriad of coloured candies, my tastebuds tingling. Maybe she would smile and say, 'it's okay, it's important to take your time,' until finally, I could breathe and make my decision.

The funeral director is smiling now, actually smiling, and it makes his face look even younger, and I realize that he's probably not even the funeral director at all, just the funeral director's son. My father did not warrant the funeral director... just the funeral director's son.

The smiling funeral director's son pauses. His words float

just above his head, like little drops of candy, like little humbugs. He pushes his pale hands through his slick dark hair. He is waiting for me to answer. I think his hands must feel slippy now, and slick, and if he were to try and open a jar of humbugs, say, his hands would be *too* slippy, he would have difficulty, for sure. So, because I'm feeling ornery and feisty and a more than a little pissed off at his stupid shark teeth and his smiling and his talking and his slicker-than-slick business-like manner, I lean forward and nod into the hanging silence. I nod toward the glass jar on his desk.

Confusion creases his brow.

'Oh, please do,' he says, with his leering shark-smile. He holds his hand for me to help myself. But because I'm apparently in the anger stage of grief, I lean back in my seat and wait. I wait and wait, until finally he stands up and walks around his stupid way-too-big oak desk and smooths his stupid pale hands through his slick dark hair and runs them down the legs of his expensive trousers - paid for with the bones of people like Mrs Ada Quinn since 1913 - and I watch him pick up the humbug jar and struggle with the lid, hands slipping, shark teeth clenched, a snarl of slipping, clenching ick, until finally the lid pops and he thrusts the jar toward me with a sigh of relief.

I peer inside the jar and say, 'Oh, humbugs, no, thank you. Do you have anything else?'

I watch him turn toward his desk and then back to me and slowly shake his head. He holds the jar steady. Ada stands in the corner of the room, eyes downcast with pity because she cannot help and she knows, she *knows*, that all I need is a little more time, and for him to stop yapping, even just for a minute, for a second, and let me breathe before I have to make a decision, but now I'm forced to put my hand in the jar and pick out one of those fucking humbugs and seethe at the funeral director's son with his stupid shark smile.

I shove the humbug in my mouth and suck hard, the

sharpness nipping my tongue, almost bringing tears to my eyes. Almost. And when the funeral director's son starts talking again, talking, talking, about colours and caskets and flowers, I keep sucking, harder. I let him talk and talk, trying to force me to make a decision, any decision, anything at all. I sit there sucking on that sombre, shit-tasting humbug, refusing to say a word or, even for a second, let that shark-faced fucker see me cry.

Ada looks on. She gives me the gentlest nod and whispers, 'you just take your time.'

Humbug Shark by Kathy Hoyle © 2023

Kathy Hoyle's stories are published in literary magazines such as The Forge, Lunate, Emerge literary journal, Ellipsis Zine, the South Florida Poetry Journal and Fictive Dream. She has won The Bath Flash Fiction Award, the Retreat West Flash Fiction Award. Other stories have been placed in competitions such as The Edinburgh Flash Fiction Award, the HISSAC Prize and The Cambridge Flash Fiction Prize. She was recently longlisted for The Wigleaf Top 50 and her work has been nominated for Best Small Fictions, Best Microfictions and The Pushcart Prize. Kathy is currently studying for a PhD in Creative writing at The University of Leicester. You can always find her procrastinating on twitter @Kathyhoyle1

11

AN EPIDEMIC OF PINK CLOUDS

BY SOPHIE LAWRENCE

Highly Commended for the New Voice Award

There is a girl in the stall next to me. I don't remember if she came in before or after I did. I have a faint recollection of her smiling as she held the door open for me, but maybe that was someone else. Now that I think about it, I am sure that was last week, or maybe the day before when we smiled at each other over the cold porcelain sinks and the cheap mirrors that make my eyes look small and my cheeks pudgy. Anyways, there is a girl in the stall next to me, and I am not sure who she is. Like me, she has been in here a while. I can hear her phone through the grainy plastic wall. Wait, I do know her. I know she has pink Converse shoes on. I can see them out of the corner of my eye because we are bathroom buddies going to the same school that costs seventy thousand dollars a year, a state-of-the-art school with state-of-the-art bathrooms whose stall walls really only give the illusion of privacy. I don't mind. There is a kinship that forms here. I think about sliding my foot across the unspoken space between our stalls, to nudge her rubber-covered pinky toe

with mine, a hand-holding of sorts. I don't do that. I almost do—
but I don't, because that would be fucking weird. I wonder if she
is actually going to the bathroom or if she is like me, picking out
little minutes of the day to escape from all the noise, the noise,
the noise. The expectations, all the ones she did not meet
because she didn't try enough, she really should have tried
harder. She should have wanted her life more, wanted it with
more than slippery detachment, she should have felt honored to
be alive, to wriggle out of the womb against all odds (1 out of
400,000,000,000,000 to be exact). She should have wanted it
like the sun, burning and bright and *passionate*. But she did not.
So, she is here with me, killing time and listening to the *wiirrrr
wirrrr-ing* of the bathroom fan drowning out all the noise,
drowning out the wet-wool texture of reality, drowning out the
overwhelming magnitude of men, of loud men, of my father
yelling. He is always yelling, mostly in my head now, and I think
about the girl next to me and wonder if she is also drowning out
her father's yelling, because we all have angry fathers, at least a
little bit, I think. It is a bit of an epidemic, maybe. My ass is
numb but I can't leave yet because the seat just got warm, so I
will stay here for a little longer. I think about how hot my ass
would get after my father spanked it, though he stopped by the
time my second brother was born (I think my mom felt bad, or
maybe he did, but that was all he knew because his father hit
him when he was younger, and that had to have done
something, made him better somehow). Now *that* was the sun,
burning and sharp and purposeful because my dad always
spanked me for a reason, he did it to teach me something,
something that made me better somehow. I sit here and think
about how my dad would lay on his back and put his feet on my
mushy little stomach and with the full force of a thousand bulls,
the strength of his military legs, lift me in the air and make
airplane noises. *Vnrrrr, nrrrrr, vewwww.* I could feel his toes
under my ribcage and I would laugh so hard and with such

ferocity that we would have to make an emergency landing on the carpet. I think about the bathroom I have back home, how I would sit in there because it had a lock and my bedroom door did not (it got taken off), and take a shit or just sit there and no one could come in unless I let them, though sometimes I can still hear my dad, the full force of a thousand bulls, telling me to *Let Me In, Right Fucking Now*, but I can't really hear him, because I am looking out the window, at the pale pink clouds just past the horizon, and then I *am* a pale pink cloud, floating in muffled blue nothingness. Later there is an *im sorry*, because he cannot help all that anger, he had an angry father, and his father probably had an angry father, and now my first brother has started yelling the way our father does, because it is a bit of an epidemic, maybe. The toilet seat is a little *too* hot now, no longer refreshing, and I wonder if it would be different if I could pee standing up, if he would like me how he likes my brothers, all rough masculine energy and camaraderie and slapped backs and football in the yard. I hear the girl next to me flush and I flush too, realizing that I have been here too long. I am a little bit stuck, actually. As the cold water runs over my soapy hands I think about his proud yells when I stood up on water skis for the first time, how his yells were so loud they echoed off the edges of the lake, how his fists pumped in the air, how his eyes were wild. And I, I remember floating on my back, the way my chest heaved great gasping breaths, the way the water's cold tongues lapped at the sides of my face, the way the sky looked spread-eagle above me, clear and cloudless and present.

My eyes meet the girl's eyes next to me in the mirror. We smile at each other, and I hold the door open for her as she leaves (maybe this time I will too).

49

An Epidemic of Pink Clouds by Sophie Lawrence © 2023

Sophie Lawrence grew up in various areas around the world with her dad as a diplomat for the US military. She has always loved stories, and when she was younger, she read voraciously. She is now writing her own stories. Her dream is to one day publish stories for other people to read.

12

BUDS OVER BLOOMS

BY CHANDREYEE LAHIRI

A category 5 cyclone warning rode on the radio waves out to the balcony where Shiuli instantly dismissed it with an irate click of her tongue as yet another alarmist misfire from the Calcutta meteorology division.

'Minoti! Bring me the leftover water in the pitcher on the breakfast table!'

She shifted her weight to her haunches with a quiet moan. The deep-squat was instinctive from a childhood spent in a home with pit toilets, but lately, her middle-aged muscles had started registering the strain. Yet there was no better position for wringing out her favorite muslin *saree*. So she paid her dues with the currency of pain, as many who love do, and squatted by the sudsy bucket in the far corner of her skinny balcony. The tiny bathroom wouldn't do; there wasn't enough space to lay it out and gently wring out each section. It had to be the balcony with its corner drainpipe that reached out its short arm as if feeling for rain, momentarily forgetting it generating its own. She powered through the twinge of guilt at breaking the rules; the housing society didn't like balcony drains to drip, especially the lawn-facing flats like hers. Water stains on the marble walking paths below were unseemly. High up on the fifteenth

51

floor though, Shiuli figured that her few splashes would disperse on the long way down and become part of the ever-present humidity. She was tired of always following the rules anyway.

This was her favorite muslin *saree*. Baba had brought it all the way from Dhaka for her eighteenth birthday. She didn't trust its cleaning to the washing machine or her beloved but clumsy maid, Minoti. When the need arose, she packed it carefully into a bucket of sudsy water and caressed rather than scrubbed it back to its pristine condition. She gently stretched it out on the nylon rope that divided the balcony into two still thinner slivers and used the special clothes pegs - sharp corners padded - to secure it in place.

She grabbed the brass pitcher she had requested from Minoti and hobbled over - her hips still creaked from that squat - to the plant in the corner.

'Oh maa! The Shiuli plant has six buds today, Didi!' Minoti coo-ed, squatting down nose-to-bud by the sinuous stem that had bored its way up through the cracked Gangetic clay. The terracotta planter was salt-stained and blotchy from a long life. It matched the tough little plant quite well.

'What do you think you're doing?! Move!' Shiuli barked.

Minoti was prodding the delicate, conical buds with a stubby finger and Shiuli didn't put it past her to squish it with adoration. She took Minoti's place on the ground and directed a short-sighted squint at the tight new buds. Shiuli almost preferred them to the blooms. So much promise, untold histories awaiting to unfurl. They would soon emerge and fan out into a halo of delicate, heart-shaped petals. The short stalk below it would flush to a vivid orange, making the petals appear even more white and pristine in contrast. No wonder it was in high demand for *pujas*, as offerings to the Gods. The wholesomeness of the bloom was almost unbearable. Predictable, dependable, fleeting. Shiuli had always favored the buds on 'what might be' before forgone conclusions asserted themselves.

It was Baba again who had gotten Shiuli this sapling, the plant she was named after, from the Rath Fair by the Chetla Bridge on her twentieth birthday. He disappeared the next year from their lives. But plants needn't worry about heart attacks and Shiuli wasn't going to lose anything else on her watch. She had coaxed thirty long years out of it, tending the depleted soil and watching the young stem grow gnarly with age. She ignored the throbbing in her right hip as she stayed in her squat to gaze on this tired but faithful companion.

It came on in an instant.

The *saree* whipped off the line, shrugging the clothes pins off with such violence that they flew around like shrapnel. Minoti redeemed years of broken dishes and chipped mugs by grabbing a fast-disappearing end and yanking it back. Yards of diaphanous fabric swirled about her head like a panic-stricken ghost, but she refused to let go.

Shiuli shoved Minoti, *saree* and all, back into the bedroom and tugged on the door to shut out the storm. The wind howled profanities in her ears, kept a firm hold on the door and sent searching fingers into the room. Minoti dropped the now-deflated *saree* and pulled on Shiuli's arm as together, they wrested the shuddering piece of wood from the grip of the cyclone. It started to close in small degrees, quaking at the violence of the dual, opposing assaults. With just a few inches left to go, the wind flipped direction with a spiteful burst. The door slammed shut so hard that splinters flew from the bottom.

The women tumbled back on the floor, defeated as much by their own momentum as by the storm. The din outside had grown deafening, but through it, Shiuli heard the unmistakable sound of a shattering clay planter. It had taken the Shiuli plant.

She sat up and reached for the shredded muslin *saree* puddled around her as the storm continued to rage on the other side of the door. Her dearest memories ripped and shattered. Literally. Then she burst into laughter. Gales of it; blowing and blasting out years of pent-up anxiety, bitterness and regret, letting it all go.

Buds over Blooms by Chandreyee Lahiri © 2023

Chandreyee is from Kolkata, India but has called the Boston area 'home' for over 20 years. By the age of 14, she had lived in 5 cities in 4 countries, so it was time. She lives in Waltham, Massachusetts and has had a long career in environmental management as a GIS Specialist. Her writing credits include Boston's 'One City One Story' (2021), Honorable Mention in the 'Boston in 100 words' contest (2020), 3rd place in Antonym Magazine's Tagore Translation contest and Finalist in Solstice Literary Magazine's Summer Short Story Contest (2023). She is also a storyteller and has won story slams (including The Moth), been on podcasts, featured in shows (including the national 'Stories from the Stage' & 'Suitcase Stores'). Wearing her producer's hat, she co-produces a South Asian storytelling show (www.offkendrik.com/voices) and curates a storytelling show for her home city, Waltham (www.wearewaltham.com). She runs flash fiction groups and public writing sessions from time to time for beginners and suffers from severe imposter syndrome. Sample her work and contact her at www.chandreyeelahiri.com.

13

LITTLE MOUSE

BY KATIE ABBOTT

Content Warning

The sun had fallen into the lake, leaving a faint shimmer over the deep emerald water. Delicate as a satin sash. The world was so still it looked like a painting. It was the dying breath of our eleventh summer, where cool evenings stippled the skin of your arms with goosepimples. We had trampled through the froth of wildflowers, still teeming with butterflies, to the most secluded corner of the lake. The twigs and bracken that snapped beneath our clogs gave way to damp, fecund earth, and finally the soft canvas of water, so far removed from anyone else that our shouts held more weight than our bodies. Lithe as seal pups, we slipped into the water. There were eight of us, the children who lived in a crescent-moon shape around the allotments. We hunted in the water for undetonated bombs, ancient ruins, secrets that grownups never spoke about but we all knew existed.

Only God knew how long he had been under. Someone shrieked. Seven of us stared, wild-eyed and shivering in the cool of each other's shadows, as a halo of hair floated in the water. A strangled sensation slowly clawed its way from my stomach to my throat.

We pulled Little Mouse from the lake just a few minutes after the sixth church bell chimed. Cradled him in our arms, water running in rivulets from his corkscrew curls. The soft blonde wisps of his eyelashes dripped. We ran our hands over his rice paper skin, now translucent and burning from the cold. Held our ears to where his breath should have been. Nothing.

Nobody said a word for fifty heartbeats. Even our ringleader, who was always the type to orchestrate group effort thefts, shrank back. He wrapped his arms around himself in panic, ribs jutting out like a street mutt's. Then, heads bowed, we began to quietly confer amongst ourselves. It was a long walk back; it would be dark if we carried him. It would break his mother's heart, and you could die of a broken heart. No, we bury him here, one of us murmured. Like the soldiers.

I remember swallowing a howl as we waded back through the gangrened water. We circled the thicket of trees for somewhere undisturbed, and finally shrunk onto our hands and knees, clawing at the earth. It took too long. We couldn't dig deep enough to cover all of his body, folded amongst the threadbare leaves, dirt caking his beautiful hair. A cross of stones where his heart would be. We held each other's hands in silent prayer. The trees said nothing, though I'm sure they cried.

Before long I'd broken into a run, thrashing through the undergrowth, nettles whipping my calves. My stomach somersaulted somewhere and I retched. It was later than late, the sky now a deep violet bruise. My muscles screamed on the bicycle as I pedaled home, sailing over the bridge where the rusted trains lay, and where the train tracks disappeared off the page into the Beyond. The world rushed by in streaks of burnt umber and seasick green. I knew my mother would be tearing the rind off apples with gusto, ready to knock me sideways with cusses when I returned. And it was Little Mouse who wouldn't show up to play with us tomorrow morning, or ever again.

The grownups called him that because they broke into smiles whenever they saw him. He very rarely spoke, as if conserving his syllables for something great in the future. He was slow in his movements too, with eyes of warm honey. Grownups told me he was "touched by the angels." I'd always wondered if it was his silence that made grownups adore him. They were otherwise forever telling us to shut up and get lost, that we were under their feet, that we complained too much. And now we had killed him when God wasn't looking, we hadn't counted onetwothreefourfivesixseveneight as we were told to do in the lake, we hadn't left when the sixth church bell chimed, we hadn't noticed when he'd slipped soundlessly beneath the lip of lake and hadn't resurfaced.

There was a milk jug filled with fresh roses on the dining room table when I returned. My mother smiled at me, then kindly told me I stank and should wash before dinner. I scrubbed my guts out with a watering can and soap. My brother had come back with a fresh new badge from the Jugend, which my parents took turns marvelling at. We sat down for dinner and my father delivered a morose prognosis of the plum tree in the garden (to be axed). We bibble babbled about our neighbours and their fat little dog, we played Black Peter and my mother won, peals of laughter rang through the corridors.

When it was dark enough to count stars, I went to bed and tried not to dream of him. His blue-tinged skin. The troops of ants crawling over his body, like the dead cat my father found at the bottom of our garden, its head crowned with maggots. It was our fault and God would never forgive us, and the meek shall inherit the Earth they always said but it meant nothing to me as I lay with sweat soaking the sheets. We could never go back to the lake. He'd be lying in wait for us. A small fist would circle around your ankle and pull you deep into the dark too. One-by-one, children would fall into the water and never return.

Now one of our bodies lay in the earth. Of the seven left, a few of us would not live to become grownups. A couple of us would leave and come back whole, but with nothing behind the eyes. Others would end up in filing cabinets. And when the first bombs fell, I wondered if he knew all along. Perhaps he knew to leave early.

Little Mouse by Katie Abbott © 2023

Katie is a writer in her 20s, living in London. This story is based on a short story she wrote in her early teens, after watching children play in a lake near her grandmother's house in Southern Germany, and hearing family members' accounts of the war. She would like to dedicate this to Mrs Wijiwardene.

PART IV

LOVE

'Giving something away is harder
when you've got nothing. Isn't it?'

Jane Eyre helped me through hard times. But convinced me that we'll find peace by using the illuminating light of love.

My fiancée proposed To me in a copy of 'Peter Pan and Wendy'. I said yes!

14

IT IS A FAR, FAR BETTER THING

BY SUSAN BENNETT

It's better to give than to receive, they say, but surely it's also better to have than have not. Who said that about giving anyway? And how do they know? They know because they have everything and can easily give things away. No. Giving something away is harder when you've got nothing. Isn't it? I'm arguing with myself again, I know, but I can't stop. I'm tired of wishing things were different, I suppose. I'm tired of losing the game and making excuses and failing, failing, failing. You're a failure, Dad had said, when I dropped yet another cup on our stone floor. And it's all you'll ever be. And you know what? He was right. He wasn't right. Was he?

I'm using up my last bit of cash (no plastic payments here) to buy my little sister a birthday present. There's bits of wrapper and fluff in my hands, too, and the gentle-faced man at the till pretends not to notice. He probably pretends not to notice the bruises too. Sure what can you do? Young family, single parent, and always - the drink. This man in the corner shop sees it all around here. But sure, what can you do? We hold each other's gaze for a moment too long, before I fake a smile and leave. The door closes with a dull thud.

Home is where the heart is and home is where my treasure is - my little sister, with her tight red curls and pale skin and a hundred freckles spread like butter on her cheeks. She's a jumping jack and a happy puppy all rolled into one, and is always smiling. How does she do it? She arrived in a tiny bundle six years ago and I immediately fell in love. I was almost ten and had never known light like this. It was as if a whirlwind crashed into the kitchen and grabbed hold of my heart and blew it open.

She hears the door and flies into the kitchen, all un-contained energy. Sometimes I think she'll burst through the walls and just keep going. Hey monkey, I say, and pretend that I've forgotten what day it is. She laughs and looks in my pockets and hangs onto my arms and stares into my eyes with such trust that it stops my heart. What? Oh yes, picked up a little something for a certain someone's birthday, didn't I? She breaks into a huge smile and runs to jump onto a wooden chair at the table. Then she rests her arms out and closes her eyes. Little sis. I want to put my arms round her and never let go. No. I want to put my arms round her and take her far away from here. Fly off (I'm a dragon in this fantasy) and land somewhere beautiful and quiet and empty. Just us two. We could forage for food, swim, rest. Hold each other on dark nights. She peeks one eye open and her smile somehow gets even bigger. My little sis. I reach into my pocket and take out the paper bag. It crinkles as she gently takes it, looks at it as if it's made of gold or as if it might explode at any moment. She takes the gift out reverently and sighs with wonder. The little bracelet is made of tiny sweets and she's always loved them.

When Mum was still around we would both get a necklace every week and see if we could make the sweets last for seven whole days. I managed it (of course) but little sis had crunched her way through them all before we even got home from the shop. Mum smiled and ruffled the red curls. Then little sis kept the empty elastic band round her neck and counted how many sweets I still had left on mine, without a hint of envy. I pinged the elastic and laughed at her shrieks as I nibbled my own sweets one at a time, luxuriating in the taste and ceremony, showing off, probably. The necklace would cling to my throat all week, ridges forming on my skin, little sis with a thin red line around her small neck. As the months passed, I started to feel strange when my neck was empty, would reach up to clutch at nothing, would search for a line on her skin.

At the table, little sis has closed her eyes and I know she's remembering. The bracelet was a little cheaper than a necklace, and she knows this too. I come to sit next to her and she opens her eyes and looks at me. Memories float in this room more than anywhere else, they cling to our necks and throats, they smell sweet, then sour. I reach out and catch a glimpse of a new bruise on my wrist. Little sis follows my gaze and frowns, lifts her small chin slightly, clamps her jaws together. I realise that she's stronger than me and feel a catch in my throat. Suddenly she grabs my arm and pulls down my sleeve, then takes the sweet bracelet and places it round my wrist. It holds the sleeve in place, clings tight, hides what shouldn't be seen. My vision blurs and I swallow loudly. Little sis simply nods once and looks into my face. We've got each other, so what else is there? Her voice is so grown up. And thanks, big sis, best present ever. She leans her head into my neck and we stay like that for a long time. Soon, our breaths match, our hearts fall into rhythm. Maybe everything's going to be all right, I think, staring at the line of pastel sweets, like rosary beads, on my wrist. I twist and turn the beads, breathe in and out, pray.

No. It's not better to give than to receive.

It is a Far, Far Better Thing by Susan Bennett © 2023

Susan is a Northern Irish writer represented by The Feldstein Agency. Her travel and health memoir is currently on submission. Susan blogs regularly from her garden shed and her work has appeared in The Simple Things and Books Ireland. She also contributes to BBC Radio Ulster's Thought for the Day. She wishes she had more cats in her life. You can find her on Twitter @shed_writing or www.shedwriting.com

15

TWO WEEKS AFTER MUM LEAVES
BY JANE DUGDALE

Highly Commended

Dad takes everything that was hers to the local charity and pawn shops, and returns with a toy that nine-year-old him always wanted but never got in 1998: a Furby.

I ask if he got any bread for lunch. He shakes his head.

I pour milk and the last Cheerios into a bowl and spoon them around. They look like little lifebuoys in an empty and calm sea. When Mum left everyone said they would help, but they didn't know what we needed.

Dad puts the new-old Furby on the kitchen windowsill, finds a fork to comb its fur and dampens a cloth to wipe its plastic features clean. He then takes a deep breath and announces that he believes the toy contains the soul of his mother – my grandma, Mary. With its white tuft of fine hair, bat-like ears, bulging eyes and beaky nose, I see some resemblance. I remember how Mum's loud words about Dad's preposterous ideas and inability to handle disagreements always followed him upstairs as he retreated from their arguments, so I say I see why he might think that.

He says he'll buy some batteries and wake her up. I want to help, so I say I'll clean the grimy kitchen window so Grandma Furby can look out. I swallow my last spoonful of soggy lifebuoys.

He seems pleased that we both have a new focus, a small, shared purpose.

Later, after the hours when Mum would insist we were productive, going to school to get good GCSEs and looking for a steady job so she didn't have to do *everything* for us, he finds a screwdriver in the takeaway menu drawer and unscrews Grandma Furby's battery compartment. He's bought a multi-pack of twenty-four Duracells, and I do not fold my arms across my chest and ask, with a tight smile on my face, what else could have been bought for the benefit of the household with the money he's spent. Instead, I replace the torch's batteries so he can see what he's doing more easily.

With two batteries inserted, Grandma Furby opens her eyes and says *cock-a-doodle-doo* and *weeeee*. My stomach rumbles and I almost ask if there's any money left, but I do not want to interrupt Dad's attempts to find the words to explain to his mother that her consciousness has been transferred into a small being made of plastic, fur and cogs. Instead of going to my bedroom and putting my headphones on, I sit in the living room and listen as everything that's happened falls out of him like breakfast cereal into a bowl – his truth about his marriage interrupted by the occasional *coo-coo-coo* and *he-he-he*.

The next day, he tells me he wants to play hide and seek with Grandma Furby. She has a program that makes her quiet, then loud, so a finder can locate her. And as Mum often said it was good that we couldn't afford to do anything as a family, because we had nothing in common, I say I will join them. I suggest going to the supermarket as there are more places to hide. Before Dad decides otherwise, I hand him his coat and pick Grandma Furby up. Together we go outside.

At the big Asda round the corner, he tells me to count to fifty before coming to find him. He then puts Grandma Furby under his arm and skips off. I flick past pages of moody, contorted women lost in glossy dreams until the security guard walks past.

Ready or not, I say to myself.

I find Dad and Grandma Furby hiding behind an open freezer door, which I close. Grandma Furby says *okay-ka*.

I find him standing on a plinth in the clothes section with one hand on his hip and the other in the air like he's waiting for butterflies to land on his fingertips. He wears a baseball cap that he takes off when he realises how much it costs. Grandma Furby sits by his feet and goes *ne-ne-ner-ner*.

I find him and Grandma Furby sitting on the floor next to a pallet stacked with packets of sugar. He dabs at the white grains spilt from their packs, then sucks them from his finger. I join in. The sweetness reminds me of Dad holding toddler-me up at the waist to bake cupcakes with Grandma Mary in her kitchen that overlooked the sea. Grandma Furby goes *la-la-la-la*.

At the end of the aisle, the security guard talks into his walkie-talkie. Its crackle sounds like Mum's voice did when she was angry. Dad stands, puts Grandma Furby in his coat pocket and whispers that we should retreat. I say Grandma Mary always enjoyed a picnic. Grandma Furby goes *weeeeee*. Dad tells me to get what's needed and meet him and Grandma Furby at the bus stop.

I lose the security guard in the sweets aisle and slip two fresh bread rolls and a pack of pale pink, square ham into my rucksack.

We sit on the top deck of the bus that goes to the village where Dad grew up. Soon there are no more pavements and clogged streets. Dad says it's time to get off. Grandma Furby says *bee-doo-bee-doo-bee*.

The sea air licks our cheeks, and the seagulls' wingtips are lit up as they circle above us. We hold hands and walk alongside a hedge until Dad hands me Grandma Furby and climbs over a fence. I hand her back, throw my rucksack over and join him in a field that ends in a cliff, above the rocky shoreline, above an empty and tranquil sea. I sit under a tree, break my bread roll in half and slap on a ham slice. Dad and Grandma Furby stand in the middle of the field and watch the waves roll onto the rocks at a distance. He is tall and upright, and we have everything we need.

Two Weeks After Mum Leaves by Jane Dugdale © 2023

Jane Dugdale is a researcher and writer. Her short fiction has been published in Reflex Fiction, The Bath Short Story Award and National Flash Fiction Day anthologies. She is currently working on a collection of fantastical short stories and can be found on Twitter @janeannedugdale and Bluesky @janedugdale.bsky.social.

16

MY SON PLAYS MINECRAFT AND TALKS AT ME FOR FORTY MINUTES STRAIGHT WHILE I TRY TO WRITE SOMETHING PROFOUND

BY JO GATFORD

Third Place Winner

It was going to be about how I was thirty-something when I realised the colour of the sea is dependent on the colour of the sky and that some seas are not just grey and some others are not just brown and the ones we can't afford to visit are not just cats-eye marble blue and 'wine-dark' was just the closest way to describe a colour the Greeks hadn't yet named, but when the sky is sunless all the oceans fall to the same monochrome void.

My son says: *You know there are probably people who lock themselves in their houses at night because they're scared of getting engulfed in pure dark?*

When a child asks what you're scared of, you say things like crocodiles and clowns and the uncanny valley instead of the fact that you are terrified every time they cross a road, and what if one day they fall down the stairs or take a knife to their own skin and it's all over in a wine-dark flood—dear God, flesh of my flesh, please be gentle with yourself—but there is time for all that and the uncanny valley is scary enough for now, so you explain how the human brain gets really freaked out about things that are almost but not quite; the might-just and the could-be.

My son says: *You know it's possible one day someone will live their whole life inside virtual reality and believe it's real?*

It's possible that when you wake from a dream, you are actually still inside of it; that all of this is just synaptic serendipity folded in on itself and maybe you just imagined everything: your life, your body, your children, your fear; the way the ocean's churn feels heavy as ancestral dread inside your guts and the way you perceive colour makes no earthly sense except that light is an ungodly thing; the way birdsong has evolved to mimic digital sound and how fucking sad that is—how ridiculous—or maybe it's all just synthesis; and maybe we'd all be happier in a cuboid world contained completely within my son's brain.

My son says: *Do you ever take so long telling a joke that by the time you get to the end everyone's forgotten what it was?*

It was going to be about—something I don't now recall. Something-something cause and effect, something-something ones and zeros.

Instead, we sit side by side and he talks at me with patient precision, explaining the properties of each imaginary pixelated cube as we dig dirt and chop wood and build ourselves a home beside a square-edged lake, beneath square-edged clouds, and when the square sun sets it turns everything—the water, the sky, the screen—some kind of pink I don't even have words for.

My Son Plays Minecraft and Talks at me for Forty Minutes Straight while I Try to Write Something Profound by Jo Gatford © 2023

Jo Gatford writes short things about strange things. Her work has most recently been published by The Fiction Desk, Cease Cows, New Flash Fiction Review and PRISM. She occasionally tweets about weird 17th century mermaid tiles at @jmgatford.

17

DAD SAYS NOBODY WINS ON THE TEDDY PICKER

BY KAREN ARNOLD

Second Place Winner

The wind blows straight in from the sea, stinging cold that makes my eyes run, but the chips are hot and salty, burning my fingers through the greasy paper. I search into every last corner, lick up each trace. Two dirty grey gulls watch from the railings running around the edge of the pier. One of them opens its beak wide and I can see the strangeness of the inside of its mouth.

Another gust rips the chip paper from my hands, whisks it out over the sea like a kite. The gulls fall on it, shrieking and tearing, a flurry of yellow eyes and beating, arm breaking wings. Mum and dad are still talking, away where I can't hear them. Mum is pale, dad's face is red. I know that up close he smells of Saturday night. I know they are fighting over me the way the seagulls are tearing the chip papers into greasy rags. Dad looks over, dares me to move. I look out,out,out and away to where the sea is silver and flickering.

Someone is watching us. The lady in the fortune teller's booth. 'Madame Leona knows all, sees all.' Mum is so pleased that I can read the words. Dad says that all these old women are charlatans. I don't know that word. I want to know but I don't want to ask. My cheek still stings from the last answer Dad gave me, so I store it for later. Mum wants to get her cards read, but there's no money left. She said well anyway, she can guess what was in the future, and sort of smiles but her eyes are shiny and bright,bright green.

When the lady sees me looking, she pulls down a paper blind and the lights go out. It is starting to get dark. An aeroplane flies out over the sea, leaving a white trail behind it. I watch it go higher and higher until I can't see it any more, only where it has been. The sadness of it sits in my stomach, hard and lumpy, like old chewing gum.

I lean against the Teddy Picker, place my hands on the plastic dome. In among the teddy bears, next to the single plastic ball with a ten pound note folded up tight inside it, there is a ring, and I think it might be a diamond. It changes colour as the lights on the pier swing in the wind. I think how pretty it would look on my mum's finger, her nails painted and shiny. She doesn't paint her nails now. They are bitten and sore and she thinks I don't notice. Deep in my pockets there is a coin in a nest of old tissues and sweet wrappers. I press it into the slot, guide the claw with chip fat greasy fingers, closing it slowly,slowly around the ring, holding my breath as it rises from a sea of furry arms and legs.

Dad Says Nobody Wins on The Teddy Picker by Karen Arnold
© 2023

Karen Arnold is a writer and psychotherapist. She came to writing later in life, but is busy making up for lost time. She is fascinated by the way we use narratives and storytelling to make sense of our human experience. She won the Mslexia prize for flash fiction in 2022. She has work in The Waxed Lemon, The Martello, and Roi Faineant amongst others.

18

HOW TO SURVIVE A HURRICANE

BY KIM STEUTERMANN ROGERS

Highly Commended

My body's a wet rag that won't dry out. It's August at this remote atoll in the middle of the Pacific Ocean, midway between North America and Asia, midpoint between here and there.

A storm is coming, and the biologist, lanky as seaweed, is concerned about a young seal, whether she's strong enough to survive. The biologist invites me into his tent, says we're safer together. This is his fifth field season, my first. He's learned a few things now that hurricanes regularly swarm these spits of land, including how to secure camp in the face of a storm. I've learned how grief can canyon a body.

I place my cot opposite his. I don't ask about the cross hanging over the biologist's door. He questions whether I'm okay, and when I don't answer, he makes sure I'm wearing my personal locator beacon.

I set up the satellite antenna, and we both send emails—me to my best friend and he to a woman, first name, Malia, last name, his. We stash important gear—laptops, satellite phone, and personal items, including a well-worn copy of the complete poems of Robert Burns that my husband always carried—in five-gallon buckets and bury it all deep in the sand.

We make one last circumnavigation of the atoll named by Hawaiians as Kauō for its egg shape, for its profusion of life, its isolation over millennia giving rise to an explosion of biodiversity, plants and animals found nowhere else in the world. Most of the seabirds are gone, leaving just the late season chicks who haven't yet fledged hunkered under bushes loosely tethered to the sand dunes. We photograph endangered Hawaiian monk seals, identifying them by unique body scars from injuries they've endured. As animals somehow know, the seals have headed out to sea where they'll be safe, but not the young one, weaned too soon when her mother was attacked by a Tiger shark.

The winds peak after midnight. Tent poles quake, and walls inhale and exhale. The sound is just like I've heard it described, a freight train, tingling the marrow of my bones, triggering electricity that bolts me to my feet, and I find myself standing in the middle of the tent, keening and wailing at the god I no longer believe in, the universe, and the doctors who couldn't save my husband. My husband who coaxed birds back to life after they flew into windows. My husband who made my grandmother's coffee cake on my birthday, because it was my family's tradition. My husband who reached for my hand as he took his last breath.

The biologist mistakes my rage for fear and pulls me to him. He mistakes my feelings for passion, his hands and tongue demanding. Rain slices through the seams of the tent as the biologist tracks the bones of my grief-shattered body, and I howl and howl and howl. His finger travels the switchbacks of my ribs to my clavicle, across to the other clavicle, and down, and I guide him in the ways that please me.

When the winds stall, my ears continue to ring. The sun is

up, and I stare at the crucifix, somehow still hanging. The biologist follows my gaze, relief softening his jaw. Sand has blasted pin-pricks into the tent walls, depositing a layer of grit over everything, the biologist and me included. The air is sulfuric, like rotten eggs. Outside, every bush stripped of leaves the way a fire takes a forest back to its bones. One wall is caved, but miracle of miracles, the tent—and we—have survived. Not so the dozens of seabird chicks, their down matted with sand and twigs, their carcasses floating in the lagoon. Marine debris litters the wrack line—a truck tire, half-buried skiff, the tube of an old television, and not more than five feet from our—his— door, a Barbie doll, her hair rubbed off, bald as my 34-year-old husband during the throes of chemotherapy.

'God is good,' the biologist says and, in his exuberance, gives me a hug that lifts me off my feet. I manage a smile and return his embrace, before everything yields to awkwardness.

We dig up the gear, and I place a satellite call to Honolulu, letting people know we're alive. Emails download on the laptop, one for him with the subject line, 'I'm so afraid.' She's so concerned. She loves him so much. She doesn't know what she and their "little biologist" would do without him. 'Please, please, please contact me as soon as possible. Praise the Lord. In Christ's name. Be safe.'

He says he needs to check on the young seal on the other side of the island, and I give him the satellite phone. I email my best friend. She replies, 'Grief fucking is normal.'

Later that night, after the biologist returns and reports the seal is safe, stars overpopulate the sky, and I take my dead husband's worn copy of the complete poems of Robert Burns to the beach, sit on a rock, and read the words he recited at our wedding. *But fare thee well my only love/And fare thee well awhile/And I will come again my love/Though 'twere ten thousand mile.*

**How To Survive a Hurricane by Kim Steutermann Rogers ©
2023**

*Kim Steutermann Rogers lives with her husband and 16-year-old dog
Lulu in Hawaii. Her essay, "Following the Albatross Home" was
recognized as notable in Best American Travel Writing. Her science
journalism has been published in National Geographic, Audubon,
and Smithsonian; and her prose in Fractured Lit, The Citron
Review, Milk Candy Review, Gone Lawn, Bending Genres,
Hippocampus, and elsewhere. Find her on social media @kimsrogers.*

19

NOVEMBER 11TH 1918

BY LISETTE ABRAHAMS

She sits at her desk, pen poised over the writing paper, its white emptiness like an accusation. The words will not come. They will not come, and yet it should be easy to write to him, today of all days, when at last there is something to celebrate. The weak November sun slants in shafts across the page, dust motes dancing in the pale light. She gazes at the blank sheet and thinks of the thousands of words he has written to her.

Brutal, beautiful words that have touched her soul.

'My Dear Son,' she begins. 'I hope this letter finds you in good spirits, as of course, we are here. The news we have longed for came this morning - Peace at last! Your father and Mary have gone to the church to say a prayer of thanks and my thoughts, as ever, turn to you.'

She pauses, unable to entirely believe the words she has written. She is aware that there is a feeling she cannot quite shake off. An unsettled feeling, a sense of disquiet. Perhaps it is because she has lived with fear for so long. In truth, she does not know how to write to him in joy. Her past letters, full of news from home, were always written with the intention of buoying him up. It was a ruse she could see through herself, sure that terror flowed from her fingers and into the ink; nonsense about the neighbours stained with an undercurrent of fear.

His letters had revealed such horror that she could no longer believe in the war of the newspapers—a war of courage, resilience and patriotism. She saw *his* war—a war of desperation, desolation and despair. He had told her that the British army was made up of boys—boys whose courage leaked as sand from the best sandbags after years of rain. Boys who marched half asleep, drunk with fatigue, their feet shod in blood.

Last winter had been the worst.

'My dear Mother,' he had written. 'I see no reason to deceive you. I have been in seventh hell. I have not been at the Front. I have been in front of it.'

His words had made her breath catch in her throat, the images searing themselves into her mind. Images of mud, and men, and her son sheltering in a shell hole in No Man's Land, the decaying body of his fellow officer beside him. The words could not be unread; the pictures could never be unseen. And the horror would creep up on her at the strangest times; suffusing her thoughts until all she could see was the bloodied battlefield. Last summer, whilst working in the vegetable patch, elbow deep in the loamy soil, she had suddenly felt the mud of France, the 'octopus of sucking clay' he had described. She imagined she was touching the bones of men, their fingers like roots, grasping her, pulling her down further and further, until she couldn't breathe, her lungs filling with water, earth and death.

Waking one morning in the pinkish hue of sunrise, images from his nightmarish world had again invaded. The sunlight had appeared as a blood smear on the wall, and it seemed to her then as he had described - that the dawn was an open wound, each day bleeding afresh.

She knew that his letters were making her ill; nervy, neurotic. And she had no excuse. She was not one of the slobbering wrecks they brought back from the Front, men who could not say what they had seen, her son amongst them, hospitalized for neurasthenia, shaking, stuttering, but safe. As he had recovered in hospital, she had made a decision that she too, would get better. And so she had taken his letters, his beloved letters, with their brutal honesty. She had resealed them, bundled them, wrapped them tightly with string and stored them away. She would not revisit them.

He had gone back to France of course. That was inevitable. The war defined him, gave him the sense of self he had been looking for. The war seemed to *be* him.

At least his last letter had been resolutely cheerful. She supposed that news of imminent peace had reached him by then. Holed up in a cellar in France, he had written in his usual blunt style, describing his situation without sentimentality, yet with an optimism that had not been there before. He almost appeared to be *enjoying himself.*

Now, she sits quietly and prays he is still there; that he has seen out the last days of the war underground, away from the wailing shells and stuttering rifles. Shaking herself from her reverie, she realizes she has spent too long at the desk, has not finished her letter, and now it is too late for she can hear her husband and Mary, returned from church. She folds the writing paper and places it in the drawer. It will wait until tomorrow—tomorrow, with peace stretching through it like a gold ribbon into the weeks ahead, with the promise of her boy returning to her.

She rises and heads towards the laughter in the hall, as the telegram boy raises his hand to the door knock. He is aware he will have to hammer hard to be heard over the church bells that are ringing out peace.

Wilfred Owen was killed in Northern France a week before the end of the war. His mother Susan received the telegram informing her of his death on Armistice Day. Whilst this is a work of fiction, some descriptions are taken from Wilfred Owen's poems 'S.I.W', 'Mental Cases' 'Dulce et Decorum Est', and from a letter he wrote to his mother in January 1917.

November 11th 1918 by Lisette Abrahams © 2023

Lisette writes poetry and short fiction. Her work has been shortlisted in the Guildford Book Festival Short Story Competition, shortlisted for the Yeovil Literary Prize, shortlisted in the Write By The Sea Poetry Competition, long listed for the Reflex Flash Fiction Award, placed second in the John McGivering Writing Prize, and highly commended in the Dead Cat Poetry Prize. Her work has appeared in several publications. She currently works as a substance-misuse practitioner in the NHS and lives in Surrey with her husband as well as her cats, Betty and Gilbert.

PART V

STRUGGLE

'I chose to believe that some babies,
like me, are born wrong.'

I would give Khaled Hosseini's *A Thousand Splendid Suns*. I find it a deeply emotional book that highlights the oppression of women in real life situations.

I'd give Marilyn French, 'The Women's Room', because it is very moving and an amazing feminist novel that changed me.

20

SUFFERING FOR MY ART

BY PIYUMI KAPUGEEKIYANA

I owe it all to Hephaestus, celestial artificer.

He is the reason I'm crumpled over on this chartreuse stool, starved for breath, fingers coated in costly pigments, basking in the adulation of a whispering crowd. The painting is my finest yet. For months, I have toiled before a live audience, working the canvas with gentle dabs, as if unravelling a scroll from the heavens. Now it is complete. For this, I have already won the most coveted accolade, the Prix du Chaos.

A review in The Old Salon reads: *The work is a contemplation on the tyranny of decay and the spectre of death. What originates as a yearning devolves into a carnival of futility, leaving only a sense of approaching darkness.*

It is a mixed media triptych, on canvas. The first panel features a wizened old woman at a picnic. She is cloaked in black, and has sunken eyes and bony fingers. I have her reaching for a cupcake positioned in the second panel, just out of reach. In the final piece, there are three young women, languid in a summer garden.

The brushstrokes, both precise and arbitrary, lend themselves to a painting with immense narrative opacity. Do we witness a danse macabre or a metamorphosis? The cupcake is almost a nod to Thiebaud but the young ladies are reminiscent of Monet's Women in the Garden. As a whole, the work is impossible to situate, transcending time and space.

What others see in it is not for me to say. I only know the price it demanded.

Take the Indian Yellow I used for the flowers. Distilled from the sparse piss of an anguished cow fed only mango leaves and water. Yet nothing leaps off the canvas quite like it, or Van Gogh would not have carved his moon with its aureate tinge. The old woman's funeral garb of bone black is derived from charred animal bones. A stable and lightfast pigment, bottomless like Satan's belly. Á la Sargent's Madame X, I added a pinch of carbon to mottle the hag's skin. See how it transforms the rose madder of health into a most virulent decomposition?

The grandmother's sombre palette conspires against the vitality of a young woman in a red bonnet. Thousands of soft-bodied cochineals prised from the pads of prickly pears, dried and crushed to make a small vial of ink. But how radiant Rembrandt's Jewish bride, caressed in her vermillion gown with its cochineal glaze. I couldn't resist dipping into it despite the pigment's fugitive qualities. That it will pale like Turner's beetle-blooded sunsets is inevitable. The very thought sends a frisson through me. Be patient, I tell the old woman. This one's scarlet vibrance will devolve into tired yellows.

The cupcake is frosted with a swirl of silk soaked in Tyrian purple. Many brave molluscs gave their lives for it. Their shells cracked with savagery, mucus glands extracted and simmered in brine. In a different gladiatorial arena, Ptolemy met his end in an aubergine swaddle, executed by the imperialist Caligula in a purple rage. That the colour of dominion appears soft and benign as icing, yet cannot shake its fetid smell, makes me chortle with delight.

What does Hephaestus have to do with this, you ask?

Well, he came to me to me in a dream, a phantasm of the night. Though hobbled and hump-backed, I found him a rare genius. He told me of his fall from Olympus and the kindness of Thetis, how he had wrought many elaborate things in the hollow of a cave, creations of which the gods and mortals were ignorant. Outcast of heaven though he was, said he'd visited Dickens with a vision of the shield of Achilles, snuck him the idea for a tale of two cities on a platter as it were, putting Apollo and the Muses to shame. He'd seen me toiling in quiet oblivion and felt a stirring of pity. Thought I was the type of man who'd understand, like Sartre, that suffering could be the raw material of beauty.

When I awoke, I knew what I had to do. Sourcing the pigments was neither easy nor strictly legal. What I couldn't find, I made myself. What I couldn't make, I bribed others to. Blindingly expensive, it was. The alchemical work alone took years.

The ceruse, for instance, I made myself. Cut fine sheets of lead and suspended them in a pot filled with the strongest vinegar. Buried the vaporous vase in a bed of fresh horse dung for two months. By the end of it, there was a chalky white patina which I painstakingly scraped, triturated and calcined over a fire. But when mulled on porphyry stone, the lead white sparkled. I used it as a base for the skin and dresses of the young women. It glowed on the canvas, with warm undertones, like Whistler's mistress in white cambric. In the process, I developed fearsome stomach cramps and splitting headaches. But the result speaks for itself.

Menandro's own cadaverous pallor is rivalled only by the gangrenous complexion of his witch, a powerful meditation on the ephemerality of flesh. The viewer is left with a lamentation on the blight of innocence.

The foliage I painted toward the end. The trees are packed with Scheele's green, loaded with copper arsenite, like the wallpaper in Longwood House where Napoleon breathed his last. It will darken with time, lending a sinister pall to the summer scene, like Manet's Music in the Tuileries. But the grass is coloured with Emerald Green, a cheerful mix of arsenic and Verdigris, more verdant than Millais' Ophelia, floating to her muddy death.

The wasting artist presents his own body as a reproach to the careless decadence of these times, an epitaph to the limits of our existence. The work shall speak from the grave with a mournful squall, a gift for the ages.

Suffering for my Art by Piyumi Kapugeekiyana © 2023

Piyumi Kapugeekiyana is a fledgling writer of fiction who is finally rediscovering her love of stories. She is a researcher by profession and until recently, had relegated herself to writing analytical articles. Piyumi was a finalist in the 2018 Bracken Bower Prize, an award given to the best business book proposal of the year by a young writer.

21

WHERE THE BIRDS FLY

BY DENNY JACE

Content Warning

I'm on the wrong side of the bridge where the pigeons sit, but I'm standing because the ledge is too narrow. I have one arm hooked over a steel girder, below the water is rough with soapy crests. Traffic was rushing behind me, on the bridge, but it has either stopped or I just can't hear it through the billowing wind. I abandoned my car. I didn't even pull over to the side. I just stopped. Left it running. Other drivers tooted at me for being a nuisance, as I weaved across the lanes to the edge of the bridge. For the first time in months, I felt calm. I didn't even raise an apologetic hand, with so much else to be sorry for, it seemed futile.

I think I've been here for a while because my body aches and my bones are cold. I deserve to be here with the birds, after what I've done.

'Lucy! Please, Lucy!' The wind blows a voice towards me that sounds like Ed but Ed is at work. Ed is the reason that I am standing here, so that I can set him free, to start again. I should cry but my eyes are empty. Tears shed in secret because they are a definite sign of weakness. A good indication that you cannot cope and if *they* find out that you can't cope then *they* will swoop in and tear your family apart. Smash up the jigsaw until the pieces don't fit anymore. But that won't happen now because I have fixed it and anyway, we will all be together in the end.

A gust of wind whooshes upwards puffing out my skirt. A reflex of misplaced modesty causes my free hand to pat the fabric down. It's thin and soft, not a skirt at all, but one of Ed's faded t-shirts that I usually wear to bed. Confusion jabs anxiety hard into my sternum. Where are my clothes? What about the nursery run? Did I dress for that? What will the other mums say? I try hard to think back to this morning, retrace my steps, tiptoeing around the huge elephant inside my head, that says *I know what you did.*

'Lucy darling, it's me. I'm here, talk to me. Please Lucy.' The same voice again. This time the wind subsides and lets me listen. My body is fixed in place, but I turn my head. Ed's standing in the middle of the empty road. Where did all the cars go? There are police with him, and a small crowd gathered behind. I didn't want to make a fuss. Ed has his arms stretched out in front of him, palms up in surrender. I go to speak but then notice that he's wearing the red sweater that he wore to his work dinner the other night. The one I hid under the bed because when I folded it up there were three long black hairs woven into the fabric. I had wanted to inspect it later, to smell his infidelity but I couldn't because Tilly woke up and cried and cried. Tilly.

Tilly

When Tilly was born and they put her skin to skin, I felt nothing. No love, no connection just the stinging pain of an incredibly brutal birth. The following months I went through the motions, kept her fed, clean, happy. I tried so hard to keep her safe, waited for that rush of maternal love, instead, the disconnect grew thicker swelling my mind with images of unspeakable things that I prayed I'd never do. I was scared to touch her in case she bruised, worried she would choke on a grape that I never fed her. And then Ed would go to work and leave me when I didn't trust myself.

Trust

Ed

Ed has someone else.

'Lucy No No,' Ed's shouting startles me. I hug the steel girder tighter. My grip must have slackened. Is that such a bad thing? I look down at the water, the current sweeping the river at speed underneath the bridge. How deep it is? Will I hit the riverbed? Will my heart stop mid-fall? Then I remember I don't have a heart.

Ed had left for work, and I had counted the seven seconds it took for him to start the car, reverse and accelerate away. I sat Tilly in a shallow bath, surrounded her with toys and ran across to the bedroom to grab Ed's red sweater. I had been unable to think straight since finding the hairs. But the sweater had gone and so I'd searched the wardrobe, the linen basket, the guest room and the downstairs utility room. I paced the floors, consumed by Ed's deceit and then I remembered. I remembered Tilly in the bath.

From the bathroom doorway it looked all wrong because toddlers sit up and splash around, but Tilly was lying face down, her dandelion fuzz of hair wet and matted, stuck to her head. She was silent. She was still. I'd imagined lunging forward and dragging her from the bath, pressing her little chest back to life, sucking the water from her lungs. But instead, I turned around, feeling released and light enough to float away.

'It's okay love.' There's something on my shoulder. Ed's hand. I place my free hand over the top of it. Our fingers back-to-front, no longer a fit. 'You're safe now, Lucy.' I consider this for a moment, relinquishing myself to him, the comfort of his forgiveness. Then he says, 'Tilly needs you.' And I realise that he hasn't been home yet. He doesn't know.

A pigeon hovers in front of me with wings stretched wide, its chest a dense dark cloud. Its claws are curled around a beating heart of mercy and there's a glint of hope in its eye.

It coo's to me, *come on, it's time to go*. And as the wind whispers my secrets to the trees, I fall out of my life.

Where the Birds Fly by Denny Jace © 2023

Denny Jace lives on a farm in Shropshire with her husband, dogs, cats and tortoise, and has been writing flash fiction since 2019. She has just started work on her first novel.

Her stories have won and been listed in Retreat West, Lightbox Originals, Earlyworks Press, Cranked Anvil, Grindstone Literary, Doris Gooderson, Farnham Fringe Festival, Mslexia, Writers Bureau, Strands International, Henshaw, Bridport Flash, HISSAC and NAWG. Published in Ellipsis Zine, Capsule Stories, Bath Flash Fiction, Reflex Fiction, Oxford Flash Fiction, Cabinet of Heed and Writer's Forum magazine.

Twitter @dennyjace

22

HOW TO TEACH AN ADULT TO SWIM
BY SLAWKA G. SCARSO

Highly Commended

Inquire about their reasons for wanting to learn now

Ahmad and I meet after his English class. We walk past the souvenir shops selling lamps and ceramics, past a little kiosk covered in Nazar Boncuğu pendants protecting you against the Evil Eye, past a pastry shop stocked with Turkish delights, baklavas covered in chopped pistachios and rose gelatines. We walk to a little café where I invite him to drink tea.

When the waiter sees us, he eyes me in a way that makes me wonder whether he's judging me, but it's enough for him that I have money, and in no time, we have two tiny glasses of amber-tea in front of us. And sugar cubes. Ahmad drops two, then, when I pretend to look away, he adds a third.

'I want to learn to swim,' he says. "Swim" is a word we studied today. Together with "boat", and "Greek coast guard", and "waves".

'You can't swim?' I ask, surprised and immediately ashamed of my surprise.

Assess their current skill level

Where he comes from, there is no sea; I knew as much. He tells me there's a river, though, but his uncle never took him there when he was small. All the people I've met at the school so far, they all seem to have only uncles and aunties. Uncles back home, who looked after them until they were ready to leave; uncles somewhere in Europe, now waiting for them to arrive.

'And you've never tried here?' I ask.

I've seen many of the refugees here going to the beach, when the tourists are gone. Some dive into the water, some swim. Many keep to where the water only reaches their ankles. Apparently, Ahmad is one of them.

Discuss any possible fears related to swimming

When I ask him if he's afraid, Ahmad shakes his head sternly, and I think this might be an easy task. When we go to the beach, however, and I walk till the water is waist high, I turn around to see him staring at me. He's stopped metres behind me and stands still, like the Buddhas of Bamiyan waiting to be shattered by the Taliban.

Establish trust outside the water

I walk back, and tell him we will start tomorrow. We sit on the beach, water lapping our feet. I tell him of back home, of the place where I work when I'm not here volunteering, of England. He says that's where he wants to go. That's where his uncle is.

Instruct your student to wade into ankle-deep water

The next day I take him by the hand and walk with him till the water reaches his ankles, and then his knees. The day after that we go as far as it reaches his waist. When he senses someone is watching us, he lets go of my hand, ashamed, only to clasp it seconds later, his shoulders immediately relaxing.

Get their faces wet

When we've mastered waist-high water, I tell him to wet his face. Before I show him, he leaves my hand, and scoops the water from the sea, splashing it on his cheeks.

'Not like this,' I say.

Instead, I bend myself till my face reaches the surface of the water. I pinch my nose shut then plunge my head. I start to sing in the water. I sing We Will Rock You which I taught him during class, that morning. When I pull up, he's laughing.

Teach them to submerge their head under water

The next day there is a storm; there are no swimming lessons. He asks me if storms are dangerous in the sea, and where does lightning strike if there are no trees. I tell him storms are less dangerous when you know how to swim–that's why it's good we're learning. Because it's the only thing I can say that is not a lie. When the sun is back, I teach Ahmad to put his head under the water. When he comes up, he smiles and throws his hands in the air. He sings We Are the Champions.

Teach the backstroke first

Backstrokes come easy to Ahmad. I tell him to kick his legs. He moves fast.

'If you go this fast, you'll get to Greece in no time,' I joke, then I immediately correct myself when I realise he thinks I'm serious.

Teach your student the freestyle stroke

Once he masters freestyle without drinking water at every stroke, I know he's ready. I make him a gold medal out of chocolate wrapping, and pass a shoestring around it. I put it around his neck. I tell him about the Olympics, that they were invented in Greece.

'Over there,' he says, pointing at the island that's been our horizon for months now.

Speak to them like adults

In the afternoons, I teach adults. In the mornings, I teach Ahmad and the other children. They all have made up ages, partly to pass as minors, partly because some have no idea how old they are. If you ask them when their birthday is, many will say January 1st. Sometimes it's hard to speak to them like children, when they've forgotten they are children themselves.

Stay positive

On August 15th, Ahmad tells me he's found a place in a dingy boat. He shows me the money he'll use to pay for his ticket. I ask him when the trip will be, then check the weather forecast on my mobile phone when he's not looking.

'When I come to England,' he says, 'I'll look for you.'

How to Teach an Adult to Swim by Slawka G. Scarso © 2023

Slawka G. Scarso has published several books on wine in Italy and works as a copywriter and translator. Her words have appeared in Mslexia, Ellipsis Zine, Ghost Parachute, Fractured Lit and Scrawl

Place among others. She was shortlisted in the 2022 NFFD Microfiction Competition and long listed in the 2022 Reflex Press Novella Award. Her debut novella in flash "All Their Favourite Stories" was commended in the 2022 Bath Novella in Flash Award and is available from Ad Hoc Fiction. Two of her stories have been published in the 2023 Best Microfiction Anthology. She lives in Italy. You can find her on Twitter as @nanopausa and on www.nanopausa.com

23

IN THE SHADOW OF SCAFELL PIKE
BY PHILIP BRISCOE

Content Warning

The last time we were here in the Wasdale Head Inn, you, me, Pete, and Tug, seems just a few months' ago, sat in Ritson's bar, drinking pints of local ale with names like Langford Gold. In truth, it is almost a year since we were here last.

The script has always been the same for our annual ascent of Scafell Pike, following in the traditions and rhythms that university friends abide by long after they stop being students. Joined by a deep, familial bond, we reminisce, and long for that lost freedom from responsibility.

They know us well in the Inn, with its tired dogs and chatting walkers still steaming from the day's walk. As the evening progresses, we become louder, shouting over each other, the same old banter, never tiring of the stories, never failing to cackle and snort at the merciless roasting that binds us. Each vying for the spotlight. To be the funniest. These are tribal rituals. They feed our spirits with the unconditional love of dear friends. We drink revolting liqueurs, some set alight, some curdling in front of our noses. We know we will pay on the climb up the mountain in the morning, but this is how we show love for each other.

Not a sensible word is exchanged all evening between us. We are all okay, right? No need to ask. Don't get too serious. I remember you were loud and as scathing as usual, on form.

We are always woken up early, by sensible, rested walkers creaking around in their rooms at dawn. As usual, Tug and Pete are first down to breakfast. The Inn serves heavenly full-English breakfasts. The best. Washed down with scalding tea. Served in crockery teapots, just like your granny did.

We stride out in walking boots, waterproof trousers chaffing together, and never enough water. You and I always look like we are wearing fancy-dress. The faux mountaineers. Never quite looking the part. Tug and Pete always looking so suited to the gear.

We park and start the ascent, Pete and Tug always pushing ahead, a continual battle to get to the top first. The alphas in the group. Pete would run it if we let him. Tug, surprisingly agile and quick for his size. You'd think he'd keel over, but he is strong as an ox. We're left to walk at our own pace. The stragglers. We tell the same jokes: have you made a will, who's got the defibrillator, and on and on. We groan and laugh as we climb and then the cardio really kicks in and we can't breathe let alone talk and we stagger, wheezing for what seems like hours. Finally, the ground levels out and we stop and turn around, swigging water and gaze down below at the extraordinary view. The lake sits in its valley, the deepest blue, resembling a dark stain against the green and grey of the mountains. When clear, you can see Sellafield's towers and the Irish Sea.

I remember asking you how you are: job, Ruth, children, if you're winning. You smiled and told me life is good. Great kids. Work is okay. Well, it pays. I follow your gaze to see what you're looking at in the distance and realise that you're staring at nothing at all. You ask me the same. We're both okay. I know now, of course, you weren't okay at all.

Back to now and here we are again. It is late September and just as warm as it was last year. Perfect climbing weather. All of us together again. This time, Pete and Tug keep close, still setting a challenging pace but they don't head off as usual. It is getting hotter, and it's hard going but we don't really notice. We are quieter than usual. Almost silent. The finality of this day, the emotion caught in my chest and spluttering out in occasional bursts which I try and pass off as coughing. Tug and Pete expressionless. I wish I had their composure. I cry easily. I find it embarrassing. Although I'm with my oldest friends, we come from a time where men don't cry, not even when they are carrying one of their own, in a cardboard scatter tube with poppies printed around the bottom, in a backpack. The last climb as a four.

We stop when we can see the whole lake below and pick our way over the loose stones and down a steep slope, scattering sheep in all directions where we are hidden from the main path. Tug and Pete look at me. I take off my rucksack and pull out the tube, which contains half of your cremated remains that Ruth told me to scatter here. She had no idea you were sad. Sad, depressed and so desperate.

I had planned to say a few words as we let you go, but I can't speak now. Eventually, Pete takes the tube, pulls off the lid and offers it to me. I grab a fistful of grit. Ground bone in my hand. Tug takes a handful and then Pete and we look at each and despatch you high into the wind so you can fly over the mountain and down to the lake below. Suddenly, the wind changes direction and we all receive a face full of dust. In our eyes, mouths, hair. For a second, we look at each in horror, but then we laugh. 'You bastard!' yells Tug. Huge bellows from the stomach, doubled up, almost hysterical as we try and wipe our faces clean. We didn't know your pain and we live with that guilt, but our friendship was built on a lifetime of joy, and we must laugh, despite everything. We smile and hug, the three of us and you, blowing around us and up over the mountain.

In the Shadow of Scafell Pike by Philip Briscoe © 2023

At four, Philip was the first in his class to read. At eight, he wanted to own a book shop with green, velvet shelves and write adventure stories. At twelve, he wrote plays and forced his siblings and friends to perform them. At nineteen, he tried, and failed, to get into journalism school because he was too hedonistic. He wants to shake that young man. At thirty-two, he regrets not applying to become a TV script reader. At thirty-nine, he took a creative writing course, however, career and children took priority. Finally, two years ago, he decided to stop stalling and regretting, and start writing. He is unpublished but has written heaps of scripts, short stories and flash fiction, knowing the only way to learn and improve is by putting finger to keyboard. He has been longlisted for one short story competition and is writing a comedy drama novel, which he aims to complete this year. He hosts a men's mental health podcast called Mid-Life Men, which inspired him to write this story.

24

THE YOU NOT YOU

BY AVI BEN-ZEEV

Highly Commended

September 18th, San Francisco, USA

'She's gone,' my brother whispers into the phone, over 7000 miles away.

There's no time to feel. Orthodox Jewish custom in Israel dictates that the body, your body, be buried in forty-eight hours or less. No exception. 'If not, the spirit becomes trapped between worlds,' the Rabbi from Chevra Kadisha explains, as though he knows what happens after death.

'Hurry,' Gil urges, but easier said than done, what with my job, finding a dog sitter, and where was I? Ah, yes, hurry. I must make it to your funeral, Mom, my *ima* or, no, there's no other option.

To-do items crossed off my list in a frenzied haze; I grab an Uber to the airport. The driver slaloms up and down San Francisco's steep hilly streets, passing a trolley with waving tourists flashing toothy smiles. How dare the sky be blue, with no infamous fog in sight?

'See? We've made record speed.' The driver comes to a full stop in front of Departures. 'I'll give you five stars,' I say and dash inside, my heart whoosh whoosh whooshing in my ears. Will I clear the scanner this time without delay?

'Step aside,' the TSA officer orders, his upper lip curled. It's the scanner. Must be; my body defies its settings.

A few questions into the interrogation, my name is announced on the PA system –the final boarding call. *I repeat, proceed immediately to your gate,* the disembodied voice commands. 'Go,' the officer huffs, and I sprint faster than I thought I knew how.

The plane greets me with hissing air vents and hospital-beige fold-out trays. My seat belt, gray and slick, clicks tightly into place, squeezing my thighs. The familiar is real but not; a facsimile of a world that once had you in it.

I can't write you a eulogy yet, but I brought a memento for inspiration—a studio photograph of us.

Look, Mom, my *ima*, there's six-year-old me, pigtailed and made to wear a dress, and look, there's you, hiding behind me, shaking from phen-fen—anything to lose weight.

'What do you want to be when you grow up, little girl?' The photographer asked.

'A bull,' I said.

'A heifer? How come?' you asked, your brow deepening its creases. You didn't expect me to become a doctor or a lawyer, but trans-species? Definitely not.

'I love to play in the mud,' I said, and we laughed, ruining the photographer's meticulous staging.

I love, no,

I loved your unarmed rolling laughter, how you kept your promises, and, yes, it took you a while, but you called me *son*.

Only seven hours after your death, memory is already growing your wings, dulling the sharpness of your horns, smoothing wrinkles, and covering liver spots—forcing a monument to motherhood constructed from the glossy marble of a tombstone.

No, I refuse the mind's propensity to lie outright.

Air pockets—a bumpy ride—and I'm holding on to my bovine childhood wish for dear life.

Mom, my *ima*, I want, no, I need to keep you gloriously messy.

The muck. I want the muck.

September 21st, Herzliya Cemetery, Israel

Damp and breathless, I join the procession already in motion— your shrunken, child-sized remains on a gurney, bouncing up and down to the melancholy sounds of the Rabbi's prayer.

Gil waves me to the front of the line, and we follow the you-not-you, wrapped in a white cotton shroud. *Liar*, I scream, no sound coming out of my throat, just my brow's sweat on my tongue. *Liar*. You swore that dying wasn't in your plans anytime soon.

Forty degrees Celsius and humid, Gil and I persevere on the pebbly path that twists and turns, the thin Poplar trees trying but failing to provide relief from an unrelenting sun.

'We've arrived,' the Rabbi announces, and we halt at your

open grave, your final resting spot.

'For you were made from dust, and to dust you will return,' the Rabbi chants, and the strangers with the yarmulkes and *pe'ot* hover the gurney over a casket-less hole in the ground. A naked cavity. Then the men tilt the gurney, and, no,
this piercing pain in my chest,
I can't look.

A thudding of stiff meat and dry bones,
   a smell of brambles, must, and moss,
   and now I do look, eyes stinging like bees,
   a body disappearing under layers of shovelled earth.
   I finally get it. You
   will never return.

October 3rd, Yom Kippur, San Francisco, USA

Of all places, here I am—Synagogue on Yom Kippur. I know, strange for a non-believer.

An ancestral calling? A homing instinct? All I know is that I'm wearing white on this Day of Atonement like you did after Grandpa Simcha died.

Far away from the home I've rejected, I look for glimpses of you in the Semitic faces of Diaspora Jews clad in ghostly attires. Greedy, I bargain with the god I don't believe in to bring you back for one stolen moment.

Stay strong, you whisper, but I could use some caretaking, a hug. I'd even hire one of those cuddling professionals—a no-nonsense lady, big-boned and buxom, who'd open her arms. 'Come here,' she'd say, squeezing me so hard I'd be forced to surrender. This woman, well, she might look like you, but you rarely hugged me, and when you did, you arched your back, avoiding pressing your breasts against my unruly buds.

'You were an unhuggable kid,' you said when I confronted you about the lack of physical affection, and I chose to believe you.

I chose to believe that some babies, like me, are born wrong.

Forgive, forgive, you say from the beyond, an absolution, request, maybe both.

You, who I miss so much, pain threatens to turn into numbness.

You, who are slipping away, morphing against my will.

The You Not You by Avi Ben-Zeev © 2023

Avi Ben-Zeev is a gay transgender man and a Yale Ph.D. As a Senior Lecturer in Psychology and a recent Birkbeck, University of London's Creative Writing MFA graduate, he is passionate about applying a psychological lens to memoir and fiction. Angel, a chapter from his in-progress memoir, Straight Femme Goes ... Poof!, won the 2023 UK's Transgender Short Story Prize. In addition, he has edited the anthology Trans Homo ... Gasp!, which was a Lambda Award Finalist, authored nonfiction books, including Complex Cognition (Oxford University Press), published high-impact articles, and has been an invited speaker at leading settings (e.g., George Lucas' Skywalker Ranch). Avi has lived in different countries, including Israel, Italy, and the US, and now resides in the UK. London is home and the location of his next book.
www.avibenzeev.com

PART VI

OBLIGATION

'She could not ask him
for her Larkin back.'

I would give Satoshi Kitamura's *Millie's Marvellous Hat* to a toddler with a big imagination! It reminds us that the best gifts can be ideas that don't cost anything but make the world more magical.

I'd give my best friend a copy of Toni Morrison's 'Jazz'. Why? Because it's the best book ever.

25

THE EXCHANGE

BY STEVEN JACKSON

How it came about was not clear but they had agreed somewhere, sometime, to an exchange of books. Of poetry, to be more exact. The book he gave was a recent discovery in an Oxfam bookshop—some thin volume of Ted Hughes. The book she gave had belonged to her deceased husband—*Larkin's Collected Poems*. They'd both loved Larkin, she'd told him.

She had taken the Ted Hughes home and skimmed through it. She had left it on the kitchen side and her youngest daughter had claimed it as her own. Her youngest daughter had learnt 'The Harvest Moon' off by heart she'd told him, and the girl could recite it all at will. You know, the harvest moon, sinking like a gold doubloon, something like that, she'd told him. Oh yes, he'd said. Something like that, it goes.

He had taken the Larkin home and stopped reading at the inside cover. In pencil was etched the name 'John Hood' in what had seemed to him an innocent hand. There was timidity in the capital 'J'; uncertainty in the capital 'H' he'd thought; and the conjoined 'oo' in Hood suggested the deepest vulnerability. He'd found out later, from a colleague, that her husband's death had been a suicide.

And how it came about was not clear but they had agreed

somewhere, sometime after, to a cup of coffee. At the Costa in the middle of town, to be exact. He had ordered a medium Americano with hot milk on the side. She had ordered a Latte. She'd asked for oat milk instead of cows', if that was alright. The coffees were on him, he'd said. The little cinnamon biscuits were complementary.

She had started rereading *Latin for Dummies* with a view to enrolling in night classes again. Her sister had recommended that she give Gaskell's *North and South* another go she'd told him, after confessing to never getting beyond the hundredth page on her two previous attempts at reading the damned thing. She'd been too young at first, and then too busy she'd said, but now it felt right for a third go. Oh yes, he'd said. Why not give it another try.

He had started rereading the Larkin, he'd told her. There was a poem in the early bit, he'd said, 'The Dedicated' it's called, and, did she know it? She'd said she couldn't remember but it sounded familiar and so he'd paraphrased the opening lines to her about the scythe cutting the grass for the feet of the angel. He'd stared at her hopefully and she told him it didn't ring a bell. And, what about the last bit, he'd said. But he couldn't quite remember the words, though he knew it was about a candle. You'll have to read it, he'd said finally. Oh yes, she'd said. She definitely should.

And how it came about was not clear but they had agreed somewhere, sometime after, to having lunch together. At the Bella Italia on the esplanade by the shopping centre, to be exact. He'd enquired about starters and puddings. She wasn't sure, she'd said. He had ordered spaghetti and meatballs and an Italian lager. She had ordered a four-cheese macaroni and a lemon soda. He'd ordered a bowl of green olives and some sparkling water too. For the table, he'd said.

She had brought with her his volume of Ted Hughes. She'd reached into her bag when the moment was right and she'd handed it back with thanks. Her youngest daughter was sad to see it go, she'd told him, but she'd ordered her a new one on the internet. It had already been dispatched and was coming in a few days, she'd said. Good to have a copy in the house, he'd said. Means anyone can have a look when they want to.

He had brought with him a mind full of Larkin. He'd memorised a few of the famous ones. He'd asked her if she liked 'Toads'. Toads? she'd said, puzzled. She'd told him she preferred frogs. No, 'Toads' the poem, he'd said. By Larkin. Oh, she'd said. *Why should I let the toad work squat on my life?* he'd begun, not stopping till he'd completed all nine verses. He'd said her daughter might like it. It's got animals in it like Ted Hughes. Oh yes, she'd said. She might.

And how it came about was not clear but they had agreed somewhere, sometime after, to having dinner together. At her house, on the edge of town, to be exact. She had googled a recipe for pesto but bought a jar instead from the Co-Op at the end of her street. He had googled 'What are suitable drinks to take to a casual dinner?' and bought a bottle of white grape Shloer. He'd also bought a bottle of sparkling wine, dispatched same-day, from Kent. He'd offered her both at the table. Ooh, definitely the Shloer, she'd said.

He had realised that he would never be able to ask her directly. He'd wanted to tell her about 'Whitsun Weddings', 'Church Goings', 'Mr Bleaney' and 'MCMXIV' and to quote from them all. What do you think of...? he'd almost asked her before her youngest daughter came in. She had asked her to recite 'The Harvest Moon' for him and the little girl had done so without missing a beat.

She had realised that she would never be able to ask him directly. The right words had failed to present themselves. Others had appeared from her lips, however, as if whispered to a ghost: ... *now you are one I dare not think alive: only a name that chimes occasionally...* and had realised then... *as a belief long since embedded in the static past...* that she could not ask him for her Larkin back.

The Exchange by Steven Jackson © 2023

Steven Jackson is a teacher and author, living in Oxfordshire. In 2022, his textbook, 'Write About Poetry', was published by Routledge. He has been published in The English Review and has been nominated as a prize winner at the Brian Dempsey Memorial Competition, the Ver Prize, and the Marsden Poetry Village Competition. He has recently turned his hand to short story writing and flash fiction.

26

SHE TURNED OUT OKAY

BY YELENA CHZHEN

We are infumed in a taxi with its meter running, waiting for Aunt Tamara to come out.

'You do surprise me,' Mum says, cracking the silence. 'Giving a dog to someone for their eleventh birthday!'

The taxi driver's eyes catch me in the rear-view mirror, re-assessing.

Maria isn't just someone. She's my only cousin. She whispered her wish in a warm puff of puppy p's into my ear exactly a year ago, having blown out all the candles on her Napoleon cake, and I said shhh Maria it won't come true (but I grinned, because I knew it would).

It took me months to save up, but I enjoyed the tactical pleasure of adding crumpled lunch allowance bills one by one towards a stack of enough. Spare change went for the newspapers. I got them from my classmate, broken-home Diana, who bought a heap from the publishing place at five in the morning, and pedalled her entrepreneurial bike to the market to sell them for a margin of a single tenge on each. 'Newspapers, newspapers!' Imagine. Anyway, she saved me the locals, which I scanned for the Cocker Spaniel ads. For weeks there had only been women looking for men, men looking for women, people selling their old furniture, and a running ad of Madam Ksenia, hereditary fortune teller solving all your problems, pay on result, 77-52-43. Until one day, Cocker Spaniel puppies, 3 boys, 1 girl, for sale, right in time! They say who looks, he finds, and I thought, are they right or what? I placed a phone call to the breeder woman, yes I'd pay in cash, and the girl was mine.

Hugging her with one hand, I rang Maria's intercom, giddy, though she was expecting me. I'm not a complete idiot. We did talk it out before, so she could prepare things. I carried the soft, dough-smelling pup up the three flights of stairs, sped past the lightless second flight where a weird man had once hissssed a cigarette out into Maria's hand when she was six, leaving a polka dot scar on her wrist, and I had practically run into her as she opened the door and jumped out.

'Oh my god!' she said.

Imagine a family movie music feel, that tender harmonic keyboard stuff, squeezing your heart a little bit — that's how it was, all warm milk and playing and feeding the puppy the food that Maria had shoplifted earlier, along with a couple of toys.

'What are you gonna name her?' I asked, stroking the puppy's silky ears.

'Lessie?' What a sucker for safe choices.

'Hey Lessie,' I tickled the puppy's tummy, and she licked my watch with her tiny pink tongue. 'Shoot, I gotta go home.'

I didn't really, but it was getting dusky and the memory of how suspended it felt to be in that apartment with its dreadful early bedtime, the memory I had from staying over once and never again, got me anxious for home. Maria walked me to the door. She pulled away after what felt like a century-long hug, and embarrassingly there were tears in her eyes as she kept saying 'thank you, thank you, thank you.'

I flew down the stairs, left hand brushing the walls of peeling paint, godly, skipping two, three steps at a time. That was before Aunt Tamara got back from work that evening and called my mum.

'She did what?' Mum said. Then she walked into my room, told me we were going, and so here we are.

The meter is wasting our time. Our money, too. Finally, Aunt Tamara, that slow cow, comes out of the apartment block, carrying Lessie in a blanket. She does not look mad, a relief somewhat, though her mad can be deceivingly calm too.

'We appreciate the gesture, dear,' she says, passing the dog through the rolled down window and giving me two pats on the head.

'Sorry about this, Toma,' Mum says. 'We're gonna take her back to the breeder.'

I hug the puppy girl and watch Aunt Tamara's lean skirted figure dance her way back to the apartment block, as we pull away. No more rear-view glances. Silly Lessie is licking the salt from my face. She's such a naive, forgiving thing. Consoling me, as if she doesn't mind, as if the short end of the stick is all mine. What an idiot, what a stupid, stupid dog.

She Turned Out Okay by Yelena Chzhen © 2023

Yelena Chzhen is a writer who lives in London. She is studying Creative Writing at Oxford University, and has published book reviews in NB Magazine, Londnr, and on her blog, foliovore.com. She is the Assistant Managing Editor at Pangyrus literary magazine. Her instagram handle is @foliovore.

27

WOMAN DRIVER

BY SAM GRAVENEY

Jocelyn hated his name and disagreed with his parents that it was unisex. Throughout his schooling, his fellow students vocally agreed with him. Jocelyn was a girl's name. In introspective moments, he decided this bullying excused his faults, and blamed all womanhood for this: were there no women, Jocelyn would, by default, be a man's name. He carried this attitude into adulthood.

Jocelyn was good with computers (something his parents praised him for), but he didn't let this stop him from outsourcing his remote coding job to four Hyderabadis. Instead of working, he passed his time running several profitable websites. This way, he became a wealthy young man. His most successful endeavour was a database of film and TV scenes where actresses were choked or otherwise strangled. The scenes were carefully categorised by actress, ethnicity (of attacker and victim), by whether the actress's character died, whether her bare feet were visible, and whether her body stayed on screen afterwards. Initially, he filled the database from his own notes but quickly built a community which provided their own site entries, and paid for membership in cryptocurrency or revenge porn, all of which Jocelyn sensibly stored on physical hard disks in his smart and clean apartment.

Jocelyn did not think of himself as any sort of sexual pervert. The site was a tribute to the actresses' talents (though there was a category for when the actress was deemed to have failed to convey a realistic strangulation). They should be grateful for the attention. Sometimes he would talk to his parents on the phone as he updated the site, and crushed his qualms. It was not his fault. He was bullied. His parents thought he was a good person, and he clung to this. He sent them photos of a dog he claimed to own; he stole them from an acquaintance's Facebook account. When his parents asked if they could visit, he made excuses.

Another of his hobbies had two parts: first, walking into a jeweller's and choosing an engagement ring. As he browsed, he would tell lies about his future wife. Perhaps he had met her travelling, and loved her free spirit. Perhaps he met her at university, and loved her work ethic. Perhaps he met her in a pub, as she sat with her grandmother, and he saw how her hands were like her grandmother's, and was transported fifty years hence, he and she in old age, old hands clasped. Sometimes he would steal the story of how his parents met, because he loved them. He thought his mother was the one good woman in the world, and his father was clever to have noticed her, far the best of a bad lot. There would sometimes be tears when he told his stories. In the nicer jewellers', he was offered champagne once he had paid. He would take the ring and the receipt. At any one time he would have five or six rings in his apartment. He kept them by his bed. He liked to look at them before he slept. Beautiful gifts, worth thousands, and by not giving them to any women, he showed his contempt.

For the second part of his hobby, a few months after purchase, he would return the ring. He would wear a dark suit, not black. He would be unshaved, but not absurdly so. He would be polite, but not friendly, and would have his receipt. The receipt would be perfectly folded, neither optimistically crumpled nor pessimistically preserved, nor would it come too easily to hand when requested. And he would resume the story he had begun. Initially, his future wives died, but he thought the shop girls got catharsis from weeping for him, and he didn't want that. Instead, his future wives revealed themselves to be shrews, or unfaithful, or money-grubbing, or cruel, or vacant. Through synecdoche, he cast aspersions on the whole female race, and luxuriated in the knowledge the shop girls felt bad about themselves as he left without a ring, and with his money back in his pocket.

As with his website, he had justifications: it was instructive. It was parable. He had been bullied, and so he wanted to show people not to be cruel. He was not a bad person; his parents loved him. If a few girls went home and were kinder to their poor men, because they had seen the nastiness that was inside all of them, what was the harm?

One day, after buying a ring, Jocelyn was hit by a car. When the paramedics pulled his jacket off, they found the ring's box, and were moved by pathos before intubating him. It was one of the first things the doctor told his parents when they arrived. They had not even known he had a girlfriend. What bad parents they were, that their Jocelyn had not let them into his life. Jocelyn's phone was smashed in the accident, and they realised that his partner (a woman judging by ring size, but they couldn't be sure) might be panicking. They were a good team, and quickly devised a plan: Lesley stayed with their boy, Aubrey took Jocelyn's keys and went to his apartment. If nothing else, his dog would be hungry.

Jocelyn heard this plan, but, with a tube in his throat, could do nothing. He did not know how he would explain the six engagement rings by his bed, or why, when Aubrey used his computer to find his girlfriend's details, it would open on the admin page of a fetish website. He did not know how to explain the absence of the dog. But one thing he did know: the driver who had hit him had been a woman, and this was all her fault.

Woman Driver by Sam Graveney © 2023

Sam Graveney is a creative writer and novelist living in London. You can find more of their work at medium.com/@graveneywriting or say hello on X/Twitter at @graveneywriting.

28

THE CASHIER

BY MALAVIKA SHETTY

He was flying in fluorescent darkness, circling languidly over the city, above the dust, the neon billboards, and the patchwork of homes, shanties, and offices - whole lives reduced to squares and circles of light.

His wings stretched out behind him, their gentle, flapping movements catching the light from below. He could go on like this forever, he thought. Here, he was nothing, a non-being— just pure essence, suspended in space with no past, no future, nothing but slow, enduring flight.

'Hundreds please,' the voice pierced, disturbing the calm, pure space around him. The darkness shattered into shards of light. His wings abruptly folded under him, and he plunged downwards, the lights rushing up to meet him, the dust enveloping him.

A check was being thrust into his face. It was that woman again. Long chains dangling, earrings flashing, face patted and smoothed into attractive order, high heels impatiently tapping the gleaming marble floor.

He reached into his drawer and took out a bundle of hundred-rupee notes. His fingers barely touched the notes as he counted them. On the notes, Gandhi's bald head with his signature round glasses flipped past, the heads merging into one another like the moving frames of an animated movie. He didn't need to count the notes. He could tell the number of notes it contained by the weight of the bundle itself. The woman was watching him impatiently. He recounted the notes, intermittently dipping his fingers into the wet sponge near him. Let her wait.

He handed her the bundle of notes and watched her red nails slowly recount the notes. With a cursory nod in his direction, she was gone, leaving traces of perfume and the echo of high heels on marble.

She was his last customer for the day. He opened his ledger and quickly added up the number of withdrawals made during the day. He matched this total with the figure of the cash balance at the beginning of the day. The totals tallied. Relief diffused the tension in his body as he added another of his signatures to the long columns of them from the previous days in the ledger. He didn't stop to chat with the other cashiers today. It was important to reach home early. Tonight, he was going to test his wings.

He stood in the train, not holding on to the bars for support. The card game was in progress but, tonight, he was not among the players. The train's motion made him feel weightless, bodiless. A throbbing feeling of anticipation and fear starting from his lower abdomen and traveling rapidly upwards to his head, suffused him.

A brisk walk through the crowds pouring out of the station, and he was home, where he lived alone, and where the trains going past his third-floor apartment still woke him up in the middle of the night. He could never get used to trains. Grim, crawly things that clung on to tracks to propel themselves forward. But planes, planes were another thing. He would never, as long as he lived, cease to be fascinated by planes. Even now, the sound of a plane overhead would make him drop whatever he was doing and run out into his narrow balcony, craning his neck for a better view of the distant, noisy speck.

He had wanted to be a pilot. His father, who had worked for forty years in the bank where he worked now and whose gold, long-service medal still hung in the china cabinet in the hallway, had laughed at him. Who would want to be a pilot when his father could get him a cushy, well-paid job at a bank which gave preference to staff relatives while recruiting its employees? In a city where thousands of people applied for a single job opening, you take what you get. His colleagues also had fathers and mothers who had once worked with his father. He had not been unhappy. Sometimes, he could even say to himself that he needed nothing more. But then, some mornings, a crow or a sparrow sitting on his would fly up in terror when he opened his window and fly off gracefully, its wings playing with the wind. He would feel angry with himself, and the urge would come over him to jump out from his balcony and fly, if only for a few seconds.

It was then that he thought that he would make himself wings.

The wings lay on his bed, gleaming dully in the gray-blue shafts of moonlight filtering through the window. It was a perfect night, cloudless, and the wind was just right. He waited past midnight until the lights in the apartment blocks surrounding his block went off one by one and the buildings became dark-gray blocks of concrete, leaving little trace of any inhabitants within. He waited until the noise of the traffic faded away, and the last train had rattled noisily into the darkness.

He fuelled the small motor and attached it to the wings. Carrying the wings up to the flat roof of his five-story apartment building, he put them on. He stood on the edge of the roof, his finger on the motor's button and looked down. The yard was empty, except for a few parked cars and a couple of stray cats. He thought of his neighbors finding his body on the gray flagstones in the morning. Mr. Colah always left for work the earliest. He would see him first.

He thought of his friends on the train, his colleagues at the bank, the shocked, bewildered looks on their faces when they heard. His finger pressed the button.

He was flying, up above the yard, above the buildings, above the railway tracks, his wings flapping slowly, rhythmically up and down. The wind caressed his face and hummed in his ears.

'Hundreds please,' the voice shattered the soothing currents around him. It was that woman again.

The Cashier by Malavika Shetty © 2023

My children's book, 'The Sweetest Mango', Tulika Books (2012) was a 2013 Highly Commended book at the South Asia Book Awards and has been published in nine languages. I am currently working on a collection of linked short stories. I teach in the Writing Program at Boston University.

END

ALSO BY OXFORD FLASH FICTION PRIZE

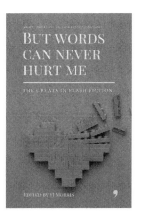

BUT WORDS
CAN NEVER
HURT ME

THE CHEATS IN FLASH FICTION

EDITED BY EJ MORRIS

Printed in Great Britain
by Amazon

29126668R00077